MÖBIUS SYNDROME TRILOGY

Book 1

CATALYST

Amanda Quintenz-Fiedler

Raven and Quail Press

Published by
RAVEN AND QUAIL PRESS
San Marcos, California

ISBN-13: 978-1-7345302-2-3

The characters and events portrayed in this book are
fictitious. Any similarity to real persons, living or dead, is
coincidental and not intended by the author.

Cover design by: Amanda Quintenz-Fiedler
Library of Congress Control Number: 2021935248
Printed in the United States of America

To my sister, Jennifer.
I am forever your biggest fan,
you are forever my greatest influence.

- 1 -

THE NIGHTMARE

This isn't real. I know this isn't real. I know that no matter what this feels like, it isn't real. I know, for instance, that the Neptune roses, with their distinctive scent, their lovely lavender color and thick, plump blooms, aren't something I'm smelling with my real nose, or seeing with my real eyes. I know this because *they* keep telling me what is and isn't real; what is the truth, and what is my nightmare.

But I don't need them to tell me. I would know because I've been here before. Twice before. I've been in this dress that I had to squeeze into because I had a little too much of the garlic mashed potatoes with my bacon-wrapped filet mignon at the rehearsal dinner last night. And maybe one or two too many glasses of wine. Not to mention the cake.

I would know I've been here before because the hairstylist pulled my updo a bit too tightly and my headache is starting. But it looks really good, so I just pop a couple of Advil and stick it out.

I would know because the same monarch butterfly is delicately flitting in the breeze near the archway of flowers and I think, *Maybe this is a sign of good luck. Maybe this time it won't be so bad after all. Maybe it'll be okay.* But even as the orange and black wings fold together when it pauses on a lily, I know it won't be okay.

They don't need to tell me because I know that no matter what I do, I can't change anything.

Here is where I turn around and inhale deeply to take in the surroundings. Here is where I see the guests, all dressed in their finery, milling about and talking to each other. Uncle Paul can be heard chortling loudly. I don't need to turn around to know that he told an off-color joke and that Sydney's friends are uncomfortable, trying to excuse themselves from his presence. Here is where Michelle, our friend who lived in the house behind ours when we were kids, comes up to me. She will place her hand on my shoulder to get my attention.

I turn, though I am not really turning.

"Hey!" she says.

Here is where I say, "Oh my gosh! It's so nice to see you! How have you been?"

I play along with the words because that is what I do here. She beams back, tells me about her job, her husband, her eight-month-old daughter that she didn't bring with her to the city and misses terribly. I let my mind wander. It isn't rude, because I already know everything she is going to say.

"That must be horrid." I shake my head. "Poor little dear!"

Now she will tell me that kids are hard, really hard, but also a pure joy.

I nod, like I did that day. I smile, I try to say the words again, give her a hug again, and take a deep breath as the string quartet starts to play. I give Michelle a knowing look and head in the opposite direction.

I know what you're thinking. Why not strip naked and streak the wedding? If it's fake, if it's just my screwed-up brain, why bother with any of it? Why pretend?

I do it for her.

Even though the tears are already forming in the corners of my eyes, I force myself to go past the rows of chairs, past the milling crowd, past the decorated white archway and into the gorgeous little cottage. I can't help but look around at the room again. It's such a beautiful little space. There are large windows draped with flowing sheers. There are comfy chairs, vanities and mirrors, and a mini fridge. The other three women in the bridal party are helping themselves to another round of mimosas, but Sydney is just staring into the mirror. I put my bouquet down on the table next to the dainty love seat and wrap my arms around her from behind, looking over her shoulder at her eyes in the mirror.

"Still time to run," I say a little too seriously. Is that what I said before? It must be. It has to be.

"Oh, stop," she laughs. She really laughs. She is giddy and nervous and full of adrenaline. She is all those things a bride is before walking down the aisle.

"Just saying."

She is biting her lip ever so slightly. It's something she does when she is more nervous than she wants to admit. It's one of her quirks I love most.

"You'll mess up my veil." She's right. I'm pulling it down a little with my weight. It takes all my effort to straighten up again. I fix her veil, run my fingers through her hair, which is curled with big, elegant tendrils. It's a shift from her normal ponytail and work clothes. She works from home, so she is often in yoga pants and a grubby shirt, because working from home means tending her garden between bouts of insane productivity.

"The music has started," I say. I want to cry. I want to shake her and grab her and run. I want to save her, but I can't.

"Hey there." She looks up at me through the mirror and turns to grab my hands and hold them. "I never thought I'd see you cry at a wedding."

"I'm not crying, you're crying." I jibe her as I lean my head back to try and convince my tears to absorb back into my eyes.

"It's not like I'm moving away. I'll be in the same house, the same drive from your apartment, the same life, just with a ring on my finger. Wait, am I supposed to wear the engagement ring during the ceremony?" Her attention switches to her finger. On it gleams a gorgeous, simple square solitaire surrounded by twenty or so smaller diamonds and a diamond-encrusted platinum band.

I use my most informational voice. "Tradition dictates you shouldn't wear it on your left ring finger during the ceremony, but you can wear it on your right hand, if you want to."

"How the hell do you know that?" She starts trying to jimmy the ring off her finger.

Here is where I lean over to get the hand lotion.

"It's really stuck on there!" She squinches up her face while trying to tug the ring off. She has been engaged for over a year, but I want to say the ring is tightening like a noose around her neck.

I hand her the lotion. "Don't tug; you'll make your finger all red."

"Oh, thanks." She puts a little lotion on her finger and the ring slides off without too much trouble. "You're really on it today." She nudges me with her elbow and rubs the remaining cream into her hands.

"Can you – " she starts. She is going to say, *Can you wear it for me? I don't want it on the wrong finger in case there's some kind of bad luck or curse or something.*

"Yes," I say too quickly.

"Yes what?" She crosses her arms. She hates to be interrupted.

"Sorry." How would I know what she was going to say that day? But I do know. "Yes, I can wear it down the aisle in case you'll be cursed if you put it on the wrong finger!" I make a scary face and wiggle my fingers towards her like some sort of ring monster.

"You know me so well." She hands me the ring, with a glare.

"I'm not superstitious about most things; you know that. I just want today to go well."

Today will be fine, I want to tell her. Today is going to be beautiful. Today isn't the problem. "Today is going to be the most amazing wedding day ever," I say truthfully.

The other three girls and I straighten our dresses and take one last glance in the mirror. I add some lipstick to hide that I have been sneaking hors d'oeuvres.

I take her arm because I took her arm that day. I walk with her to the designated spot, her wedding planner on a headset waving her hands for us to stop before the crowd can see us. Sydney grabs my arm more tightly, taking a deep breath.

"Let's…," I start.

She looks up at me. Her smile is so blissful. She is so happy. This is how I remember her. This is how I want to remember her.

"Let's what?" She is practically giggling.

I want to say, *Let's get the hell out of here. Let's run. Let's steal a fancy car and drive off like Thelma and Louise, but without all the crime and death.* What I do say is, "Let's go."

The music changes from something lovely but unrecognizable to Pachelbel's *Canon in D*. It may be overused in these situations, but it was our father's favorite. It's a way for him to be here, even though I am in his spot. It's a way for us to remember. The lavender roses are for our mother. She, too, is absent from the event, passed on like our dad. Before I let that thought overtake me, I think of the beautiful roses in my hand. I fiddle with the ring on my finger; it feels foreign and too heavy.

I take a last breath before we step forward, turning the corner to see our friends and family standing and waiting for us, for her. She lights up as the crowd murmurs in awe. She is a vision, taller than me by a few inches, but I found particularly high heels so we would be about even. I also made sure to convince her to get low heels so she would be comfortable, a slight manipulation on my part to even us out down the aisle. Everyone is beaming. Sydney is glowing.

I jab my thumb onto a thorn in my bouquet. I push it on, hard, until I feel a drop of blood slide down my hand. It is the only way I can keep myself grounded enough not to leap up to the altar and strangle the man responsible for everything. I want to remember her happy. You have to understand that.

I release her arm, careful to be sure the blood doesn't drip on her gorgeous art deco dress, and I let her go. I let him take her hand. I let it happen. And now she's dead.

- 2 -

THE REAL

I wake up shaking, my blood has gone cold. The nurses are fussing over their machines. One I don't recognize is looking down at me, trying to get me to see her through the fog of the lapse.

"Taylor, Taylor, can you hear me?" she asks. I try to reply, but my body is not yet mine again. I can feel the tingling through my skin, the throbbing in my veins, and my head is pounding. All of my nerves must have been firing at once. It's a violent thing, to lapse – seizures, blood pressure alternating between hyper- and hypotension, my temperature falls dangerously low, my pulse varies between rapid and almost indiscernible.

You can imagine I am a bit of a mystery for the medical staff. They have been trying to diagnose me since the accident. It's obvious I have some sort of brain injury, but nothing quite describes my condition correctly. It isn't epilepsy, even though I have seizures. It isn't schizophrenia, even though they are trying to determine if my "memories" are hallucinations. It isn't Parkinson's or Alzheimer's or a brain tumor. In fact, they can't tell me what the hell is going on at all. The only thing they can tell me is that I can't leave this place. This facility is meant to keep me, and others, safe from my episodes. But they can't keep me safe because they don't know what's going on.

My room is small, but it's mine. I have a bed that is bolted to the floor, a night table that is an extension of the bed, and a cheap sconce screwed onto one wall, presumably to prevent me injuring myself or someone else by accident. Or on purpose, I guess. It's one of the many things that remind me I don't really have any control here. And why should I? I can't even control my mind.

The nurses stay with me until all of my vitals have returned to normal. Well, my normal. I do have hypertension, which isn't helped by my current situation. I also suffer from anxiety and depression, so, yeah, I'm in a pretty shitty predicament. Everything that can be diagnosed is being treated, but I can't get out of my funk when I can barely get out of my bed.

Almost as if on cue, Dr. Strove comes in with his clipboard, flipping through his notes, his consternation forever written across his forehead.

"Hello, Ms. Donlan." He doesn't even look up anymore.

"Hey, Doc. Any chance you're going to call me Taylor today?"

"No." He is used to the question. I don't use it all the time, just when I think he might actually bend his rules. It would be nice if I felt a little human in this place.

"Another lapse, I see." He frowns. That's what he calls them. My hallucinations, memories, violent episodes – to him they are lapses. He doesn't know what else to call them. "This is troubling."

"Tell me about it."

He looks up this time. I almost don't know what to do. I'm not used to him looking at me. I plaster on my biggest grin. He grimaces, then takes a deep sigh. "This lapse was particularly concerning."

I break eye contact. It's too real, too personal. I know, I know, I'm probably dying of something new, something undefined, something that no one has ever heard of or will ever see again. There is no reason to think about it too much. There is clearly nothing I can do. "Concerning, huh?"

"Yes." He is a very matter-of-fact man. No bedside manner to speak of, but at least he tells me the truth. "You had a serious seizure and your heart, kidneys, and lungs were all severely strained. Your temperature was within a few tenths of being hypothermic. Not to mention the brain stress that is undoubtedly occurring during each lapse. Your brain chemistry is starting to concern me more. I need to be able to study it more closely, but that is difficult since the lapses are so unpredictable."

He sighs. It's a deep, tormented sigh. He's used to being able to solve people. Solve their chemical imbalances, rewire their minds to avoid trauma, circumvent damaged areas. All in all, he saves lives. He gives people back a real life. He is almost as frustrated as I am that he can't solve me.

* * * *

My routine is pretty absurd. I can't move too far from my room for fear I will have another episode. I have to stay attached to lots of machines, mostly to monitor that I'm not dead yet. I drag them around on a pole. There is a game room, but the other people in this long-term facility are not really familiar with Exploding Kittens, and I don't play gin rummy. Besides, the game room is mostly empty and the cathode ray tube television suspended from the ceiling doesn't even get fuzzy broadcasts anymore. None of us are really well enough to want to pretend to be having fun. It takes too much energy.

Food is brought to me on a little tray table on rickety wheels that fits over the bed, which means I eat in bed. I hate eating in bed. I always feel like there are little crumbs all over me and that I'm somehow getting slimy. I never used to eat in bed before all of this. It was forbidden in my bed, and led to more than one romantic interlude ending prematurely in someone else's. It is one of my biggest pet peeves. Yet they won't let me take a tray to the game room. It's against protocol, they tell me. It might upset the norm (like there's any normal here to be screwed with).

Even though I'm relatively healthy, young, and lively, I am stuck here until they figure this out. I can't be released, I'm told, because I don't have a family member to care for me and I can't afford live-in help. My insurance was crap to begin with, so this is the most I can manage. The most I will ever be able to manage. And I might eventually lose this as well.

I don't see why they care so much. I think, at first, I was an interesting challenge for Dr. Strove. He wanted to find out what would cause this. Not for fame or even for the greater good. For him, I think it's just a matter of pride. He doesn't like to lose, and he seems to think I have something to do with what is happening. Not that he doesn't believe me, because most of my symptoms are impossible to fake, but he just has this look about him like I'm messing with him. It's the only fun part of my day.

* * * *

The facility itself is designed for epilepsy in the elderly. There are nurses around the clock in a central station. The patients all have individual rooms, which I guess is one silver lining. A roommate amidst all this other stuff would be an even greater horror show.

It was designed with a simple, economical approach. The walls are a grayish white, the faux marble linoleum floors go a few inches up each wall for ease in cleaning, and the furniture is sturdy and sterile, if not particularly comfortable. There is a small, stout bookshelf in the game room that holds a few well-worn books and easy board games in cardboard boxes held together with tape at the corners. There's a Sorry! game – which I personally find insulting, as if it's chiding my existence – and checkers, Connect Four, and a chess game where at least three of the pieces have been replaced with action figures from Happy Meals.

There is no other gathering point for the patients, though there is a staff break room. Sometimes I can hear muffled conversation and I yearn to barge in and demand that they treat me like a human, too. I'm younger than some, older than others, but I have a lot more in common with them than my aging cohabitants.

I've never been good at making friends, anyway, so it's not like I have the skills to march in and charm them into friendships. Even if I could befriend them, the nurses have a pretty high turnover rate. Either they're finishing some sort of training, which often seems to be the case, or they're so compassionate they get attached to the elderly patients and are heartbroken when they lose too many, or they were stalled in this place while they sought better gigs. That's not to say that some of the nurses don't choose to be here, but the senior staff have all become leaders and heads and chiefs of whatever they do. Meaning I don't see the same people very often or for very long.

I have been here for months. I don't know how many because I stopped keeping track of time when I realized it was pointless and painful. I'm here for the rest of my life.

- 3 -

REMEMBERING

Sydney and I had been best friends for as long as I can remember. I know that sisters think that all the time, either that or they seem to be enemies from birth. But Sydney and I, we really were best friends.

We lost our mother to brain cancer when we were young, I was only six and Syd was nine. I have these wonderful memories of her gardening in her rose bushes, or swimming off the edge of a pontoon we would rent at the lake. I remember she had kind features and a boisterous laugh. I also fill in the missing bits with stories from other people. Our father would tell us fanciful tales; how she would do silly little dances to make us giggle or how she loved the stars so much she would sleep outside sometimes, even when the weather turned too cold for her to stay out all night. They were magnificent stories, but they were all I really had.

When we lost our father to a sudden heart attack, I was already out of college and had lived a life with his presence. He was this anchor of a man who devoted his life to his work in virology and to me and Sydney. There were times when I wondered if he didn't love tiny viruses more than us, but not Sydney. She always looked at him like she was seeing a superhero, and that no one else could see through his disguise.

When he died, Syd and I became even tighter. We lived together in our childhood home while we tried to work out how to sell it. We spent almost all our time together. We tried to figure out how to carry on without a foundation. So, we became each other's foundation. We lifted each other up, supported each other's endeavors, helped correct each other's flaws and faults, and we survived.

Back then, in the year or so after his death, we would take turns losing it completely. We seemed to always know when the other was about to crash. Without warning, to most people, the crash would overcome us. We would weep uncontrollably on the floor of Target. We would go binge drinking to drown the feelings that were too unbearable. We would catch unsuspecting men, use them up, and return them to the wild. We self-medicated, we were promiscuous, and we were emotional – but never at the same time. When one of us would be weeping in the linen aisle, the other was there to comfort her and give knowing glances to concerned passersby. When one of us was on a bender, the other was wingman, chauffer, security guard, and support. We were always safe with strange guys and never went home with them, but would bring them home with us, where the other one of us would chase them out in the morning with withering glares and unsubtle commentary.

I like to remember those times. Back when we had each other's backs in all things. In this place, where I am separate in so many ways, I like to remember. You would think that memory would scare me, but memories are harmless and wonderful things we can carry with us. The lapses, on the other hand, are wrenching and painful. They aren't things that you think in your mind's eye, they are lives lived in caustic detail. Every sight, every smell, everything you experience in the real comes back to you in a lapse. You are so fully in the lapse that your body reacts. With violent intention, your body tries to keep up with your mind – tries to keep you alive. Without the guidance of your brain, though, the body is a fish, flopping on the deck of a boat with no real chance of getting back to the water.

* * * *

From the time we were teenagers, Sydney and I were boy crazy. I like to pretend it was on my 13th birthday that we went to the mall to gaze at the variety of high school guys and swoon, but truthfully it was probably closer to my 15th. We would pick a couple of boys to dream after every few months or so. Even though she was older than me, we were almost always together. Without our mom, I think she felt the need to make sure I had female support, and when we were teens, that meant someone to talk to about boys.

I noticed early on in our adventures that she was catching the eye of more than one of our fantasy boys. A few even asked her out, ignoring that I was even there standing right next to her. But she would feign disinterest and loop her hand through my arm and drag me away. Then we would talk about how great his hair was, or how he probably had a six-pack, or his dreamy eyes.

I would have leapt at the chance to date any one of her admirers, but Syd just ignored them. It wasn't until she was in college that I discovered that not only was it harder to get a guy's attention than she made it seem, but we had very different taste in guys. She had this thing for guys that were smart and a little arrogant. They were usually well put together – well dressed, fit but not overly athletic, short hair, clean-shaven faces – whereas I went for the guys that were free spirits – artists, skaters, musicians, those few athletes that wanted to break free from their rigorous schedules and take a walk on the wild side. In retrospect, considering me, the idea of the wild side is hilarious. Aside from lots of ear piercings, a quaint tattoo on my back, and freedom with my hair color and style, I was pretty straitlaced.

But where Syd and I differed on the outer presentation of guys, and even some of the inner motivation, we always had one thing in common – the guys had to respect us and our intelligence. We were both A students, hard-working and ambitious, and we had no time for guys that were condescending, dismissive, or generally jerks.

Which is why, even today, I don't understand how it all happened. If we hadn't gone to that bar that night and been tipsy enough to sing "Poker Face" at the top of our lungs during open mic karaoke, and if she had seen how he treated her, how he treated me, instead of looking past that and believing his phony smile, then maybe everything could have been different.

- 4 -

RELEASE

I don't want you to think this was planned.

None of this was intentional.

I am not in control of my life.

There is nothing I can do but wait to lapse or die. I just want to get out of here, however I can. No matter the costs or consequences.

This place is more medical facility than residential accommodation. The nurses come and go, entering rooms through continually open doors without even knocking. And there is a different one every day as the dozen or so staff rotate patients and shifts, and some rotate right out of the facility. Even the ones I have seen more than once are all business and have no patience for my off-the-cuff remarks and small talk.

Aside from the turnover in the nursing staff, the residents are never here for long, either. They are elderly to begin with, so some of them pass naturally. Some of them find solutions to keep them safe and manage the seizures, thanks to Dr. Strove. Those lucky few get to go home to their loved ones. Others go from here to hospice. None of them stay here too long.

And that makes Dr. Strove my best friend in this place. Not because he is kind – he won't even call me by my first name – and not because he is particularly interested in me as a person. But rather, Dr. Strove is my best friend because he is the only person with whom I have a lasting relationship. He has been with me since this new beginning. He knows my chart inside and out. He watches me and monitors me and keeps tabs on me, even when he isn't here. Sometimes the nurses are called in the middle of the night to check in on me and take a vial of blood, or my blood pressure, or a urine sample. He doesn't tell me what he's looking for, but I imagine him sitting up in bed in the middle of the night with a new idea that just can't wait until morning. So, in his own way, he is working for me. He is trying. That makes him my best friend in this place.

But that is not enough.

* * * *

The sconce is old, yellowed plastic. It isn't pretty. In fact, it is barely functional, as the years of aging have caused it to block a good deal of the light from the bulb. But it does have two helpful characteristics. One, it is within reach of my right arm, which does not have the blood pressure cuff that inflates every half hour or so throughout the day and night. And two, it has become quite brittle.

I've watched the new set of nurses and I understand their basic routine. After Nurse Curly-Hair checks in at the desk with Nurse Purple-Nails, the two of them go check on another patient, someone I don't know who apparently needs two nurses to manage him. Even though Nurse Handsome-Guy should be at the desk when they leave, he takes too much time with each patient – he's pretty new to this – and that should give me fifteen minutes or so of time between nurses at the monitors.

So, I quietly get out of bed and creep to the open door to get a better view of the scene. Here comes Nurse Curly-Hair to check in. I am watching the nurses' station too closely and Curly turns to look at me when Nurse Purple-Nails – no wait, now they are bright green – points in my direction. I wave nonchalantly and return to my bed to sit impatiently on the stiff mattress. They have a conversation, clearly about me, but then Nurse Now-Green-Nails shrugs and they head off to the mystery patient. No sign of Nurse Handsome-Man.

Now's my chance.

I quickly get up and rush to the light fixture on the wall. The sconce breaks pretty easily with enough pressure on the weakest point of the aged plastic. I have to catch as many of the pieces as I can to avoid too much clatter. A quick look out my window to the hall tells me there are still no nurses, and no one seems to be running to see what the noise was. I lower the other pieces onto my bed and find the sharpest three.

Now I know what you're thinking. I know this sounds too drastic. There has to be hope, right? I just don't see it. I am dying already of an undiagnosed nightmare disease, so I'm going to take this last, final control of my life. Sydney is gone. My parents are gone. My friends have abandoned me, and Dr. Strove isn't enough.

I'm a smart woman. I realize that to do this I will have to work quickly and definitively. Even though I know this, I hesitate over my left arm. I'd have to cut through a decent amount of scar tissue from a horrid burn I got as a child. That isn't going to be easy. I switch the shard into my left hand, even though I am right-handed, and it feels awkward.

I stab the shard into my arm near the elbow and shove it with all my strength down the length of my arm to my hand. I can't grasp it with my right hand now, and it seems like some might have broken off in the wound.

I fall to my knees. I should have started on the ground. That was stupid. Only one arm won't do it, so I stab my leg where I think the femoral artery is. There is a lot of blood, but I don't know how much is enough. I try to cut here, too, but it's too painful and I'm getting light-headed. Not from the loss of blood but from the act itself. I can picture Sydney screaming at me, shaking me and weeping. *Why, why would you do this?*

"I have to," I say to no one.

Syd would run her fingers into her hair and grab it, hard, at moments like this. Moments where everything is spiraling out of control. She did that very thing before she got into the car that night, crying and yelling and grabbing her hair.

It's too much to think of – how upset she would be. How much terror and anger she would have, unable to stop me. I can't think about her anymore. I need to end this quickly.

My throat, I think. *I can stab my throat.* But I am having trouble with staying focused. There is a lot of blood. It's hot and starting to get sticky. I try to raise the shard with purpose. Try to jam it into my weakly throbbing jugular. I think I manage a cut, but nothing significant.

The funny thing about Dr. Strove is that he has no real routine. He is a very clinical, rule-abiding guy, but he also marches to his own drummer. Of course, I had no way of knowing when he would walk by. But I still had to take a chance.

I had to.

Dr. Strove is stronger than he looks. Everything now is soft around the edges, but here he is, coarse and sterile and strong. He is moving quickly. He is shouting, I think, but I have chosen to tune it out. I have gotten good at tuning things out in my lapses; I'm well practiced. He is going to ruin everything. I try to shove him away, but somehow two nurses have come in without me noticing. One is holding something to my right arm. The other is trying to restrain me from swinging at Dr. Strove.

"No," I beg.

It's Nurse Handsome-Man. He is sallow and keeps swallowing hard. I can't tell if he's not sure what to do or if he has a thing about blood. I try to ask, but nothing comes out.

With my free left hand I grab Dr. Strove's jacket. It has drops of blood decorating the front in all sizes. It's sort of beautiful.

"Please…" I try a smile.

"Stay with me, Ms. Donlan!" He is clearly screaming, but it is just a whisper now. I shake my head. "Stay with me, Taylor," he continues.

I smile for real this time. "Does this mean we're friends?"

Everything goes blissfully, completely bright, quiet, and calm.

- 5 -

CONSEQUENCES

I should have realized that things could get worse. Now that I have been classified as a danger to myself, I'm strapped into bed and monitored more closely. So now I can't even move around with the modicum of freedom I had before. Consequences.

It's been a week and I've been in and out of consciousness. Some of it is drug induced, I think, and some is because I have given up. I would love to just fade away, like Michelle Pfeiffer in *Dangerous Liaisons*. Just to die of heartbreak and grief; that would at least be something. A little dramatic for my taste, but it would certainly solve the problem of my earthly damnation.

The other consequence is that Dr. Strove doesn't come in as much. He sends the nurses a lot more, the ones that are still around. Nurse Handsome-Man is gone. I hope he didn't get fired on my account because he wasn't at his post, but it might be for the best as he looked awfully squeamish the last time I saw him. Dr. Strove's absence is a consequence I didn't expect. And I didn't know how much I needed that one little semblance of normalcy, of regularity. If you have one thing in your life you can count on, you can look forward to something, expect something, know one segment, however tiny, of your life to come.

Now he doesn't come. Now he walks along the far corridor, on the side of the nurses' station that is furthest from me. I have forced my only friend to the far side of the building – the far side of my world.

* * * *

It is a genuine shock to wake up to the restraints on my wrists being loosened. Of late, even when they are changing my bandages, they don't fully loosen the restraints; just sort of move them around different parts of my arms.

I decide to open my eyes after a bit of trepidation. Looking at the angry nurses makes everything harder, but when I see his face I gasp a little. He pretends not to notice, though the way he turns away from me suggests he doesn't want me to see his expression.

"I've missed you, Doc." I try to hide the slight cracking in my voice. I haven't spoken in a few days.

"I doubt that very much," he says, way more quietly than normal.

"Lemme guess, you're sending me to a farm upstate."

He generally doesn't like jokes, but this time his shoulders sink a little. I didn't expect that, either. I didn't expect that he would be wounded by my actions. Consequences.

He walks out of the room and I can barely hear him say, "Come with me."

I haven't stood for a week or more, so this seems uncharacteristically risky on his part. I can see Nurse Now-Orange-Nails scowling at me, certainly keeping an eye on me, but not coming in to help.

As I swing my legs over the side of the bed, I realize that most of the equipment I haven't been able to escape from is disconnected from me. The catheter is gloriously gone, but so too are the IVs, the blood pressure cuff, the pulse monitor, the little sticky circles and wires that felt more like chains than monitors – it's all gone. I have a small device wrapped around my wrist, which looks like a blood pressure monitor, but smaller and without wires. That, my thin gown, and the remaining bandages are all I have that indicate I'm a medical patient of some kind.

My legs are wobbly, but not without some strength. By the time I manage to get up and slowly make my way to the door, Dr. Strove is out of sight. I only know he turned left. Left is where the game room backs up to the employee lounge. Left is where there are four other rooms that have patients I've never seen, behind curtains and closed doors. Left is the door to the stairwell that leads to the lobby that leads out of the building.

I look to the nurse and she just crosses her arms and scowls more.

Okay, I deserve that, I think as I make my way along the wall, heading to I don't know what.

It takes me longer than I would like, but at least I am out of bed. At least I'm moving and seeing something more than the dark walls of my room. The always-dark walls. They haven't replaced the sconce, for obvious reasons, and when they need a light, they have a clunky monstrosity on wheels that they roll through the door, clumsily, and plug into the wall. Then they wheel it out again, leaving me mostly in the dark.

I start to feel like I'm walking towards a lobotomy. Perhaps they are going to cut out the part of my brain that makes bad decisions, to leave me without the ability to make any decisions. I pause in the hall. Not because I can't go forward or I'm weakened from the walk, but because I have a sudden burst of irrational fear. Fear that I am being released because they cannot help me, or maybe I voided my insurance with attempted suicide, or somehow they have decided I'm not treatable, or not worth treating.

I look over my shoulder towards my room and take a deep slow breath. No matter what, it can't be worse than the last few weeks.

* * * *

I finally make it to the end of the hall, where I look around for any sign of Dr. Strove. I am about to head to the stairwell, certain at this point that he is kicking me out, when I hear the soft tenor of his voice coming from the game room. I head over to the room and see Dr. Strove, his back to the door, seated at one of the three small game tables with an older woman I don't recognize. She is smiling at him and they are having a conversation. A real conversation.

"Trying to make me jealous, Doc?" I say without thinking. I am jealous. This is what I have wanted, from him, from anyone, for months.

The woman's happy expression fades and she stares at me as if sizing me up. Dr. Strove doesn't turn around.

"Ms. Donlan, I'd like you to meet Ms. Griffin."

"Howdy." I try to hold down my resentment, but I am not adept at hiding my emotions on a good day. Today is not a good day.

She takes a deep breath and sighs, looking from me back to Dr. Strove. She shakes her head almost imperceptibly. He takes her hand in his and says something too quiet for me to hear. I might not have heard it even if he had shouted, though, because he took her hand. He reached out and comforted her and all sense I had of my surroundings diminished to only that action — his hands clasped around hers. I steady myself on the doorframe, unfamiliar with this level of envy. I don't even really like Dr. Strove. And he certainly doesn't like me. So why am I so hurt by this one small gesture of friendship between him and this stranger?

Dr. Strove stands and pulls the chair out. He gestures to it without looking at me. I can't remember the last time our eyes met.

I steel myself for the journey to the middle of the room and try my best to ignore him as he is ignoring me. The tears forming in the wells of my eyes are harder to hide, but as long as he doesn't look at me, he will never know.

* * * *

We stare at each other for a few minutes after he leaves. Not only was Strove friendly with her, but she is wearing a gold chain that disappears under her shirt. I have not been allowed that kind of freedom. Even though

I don't have something like that to wear, I know that if I did I wouldn't be allowed to and that, alone, makes me even more angry. My animosity must be written all over my face. Ms. Griffin finally crosses her arms and leans back in her chair.

"Well, aren't you going to say anything?" She sounds impatient.

"Such as…," I inquire while shrugging.

"Are you trying to be difficult? This is a huge gift he's given you."

I cross my arms in response. "Yes, a great gift to be let out of my restraints so I can walk forty feet to sit here with an angry old woman."

I jerk a little when she unexpectedly laughs.

She shakes her head. "Oh, hell, girl, you have no idea. It's a big deal that he is even letting you stay here at all. Do you know what he had to do to keep you here instead of letting the state lock you up in the psych ward at County?"

"No," I reply sheepishly. "Do you? No one has told me anything."

"Can you blame them?" She leans forward on her elbows, looking at me so intently that I feel like she is looking through me, like she can see the things that make me up and they are insignificant.

"Fine." I slam my hands on the table. "I screwed up. But can *you* blame *me*? I've been stuck in this place for longer than I even know with no sign that I am getting better, being treated, even being diagnosed with anything. I cannot stay here forever!"

"Carrie," she interrupts.

"What?!" I can tell my blood pressure is rising. "Like, the Stephen King book?"

"What? No, you idiot, my name is Carrie."

The monitor on my wrists starts beeping slowly.

"What? Who *are* you? And if you say, 'I'm Carrie,' I'm going to blow a gasket!"

The monitor starts beeping more rapidly.

"You might be right about that. Take a deep breath, kid." Carrie reaches out and gently grabs my hands. It's such a simple gesture, but I start sobbing uncontrollably.

I can hear the nurses, at least two, run into the room, but Carrie raises one of her hands and shakes her head without taking her eyes off of me. I try a couple of deep breaths through my sobs and the beeping slows and finally stops.

"So they *are* still keeping tabs on me," I finally manage to say, wiping sloppy tear streaks off my face.

"Of course they are, kid," Carrie says with a kinder tone. "He hasn't given up on you even though you have given up on yourself."

"Of course he hasn't." I shake my head. "I haven't been *solved.*"

She leans back, biting the inside of her cheek like she's chewing on a thought. "I grant you, he likes a good puzzle, but in your case, I think he's kind of fond of you."

My laugh turns into a snort as I pull away from her and sit up straighter. "Now I know you're lying."

She shakes her head. "I know he seems distant, and he is always the professional, but he works on your case all day every day. He asked me to come here, at great personal expense, mind you, just to try and help you."

"He paid you to be here?" I shake my head again. Of course he did.

"What?"

"You said 'great personal expense'," I parrot, not even trying to keep the anger out of my voice.

"Oh, no. I mean *my* great personal expense. I don't want to be here. But I will do whatever I can to help him. You, I'm not sure I care about helping just yet."

I look up at her again. "So he didn't hire you?"

She shakes her head. "Hell no. I'm a resident."

Even though she was certainly near the same age as most of the patients here, she seemed more in control of her faculties and in much more vibrant shape than the others I have seen.

"You get seizures?" I ask skeptically.

"No," she says. "I used to. He cured me, or, at least, made my life livable again."

"So why are you a resident here?"

"Enough about me," she says in a dodgy way. "You need a friend, kiddo."

"Yes, that would be nice, but what I really need is to get out of here."

Carrie scratches her chin thoughtfully. "Yeah, I get that. But until then, you need to make do with what you have."

My laugh sounds almost cartoonish, like some sort of evil villain cackle. "What I have. Right. Let's see, what do I have? No personal freedom? Check. No decent entertainment? Check. No communication with the outside world? Check. No hope for the future?"

"Check, yeah, I get it." Carrie waves a hand at me dismissively. "You just have no imagination."

"Imagination." I scowl. "So, you want me to pretend I have those things? Won't that lead to some sort of mental breakdown?"

Carrie sighs in an exaggerated manner and shakes her head. "I'm starting to think you want to be difficult. Come with me."

"Everyone's being bossy today," I whisper to no one in particular.

Carrie heads to the window of the game room. "Well, come on, then!"

My dramatic sigh matches hers and I join her at the window. "Yes?"

"What do you see?"

I snort a little. "Um, a tiny sliver of sky, an office building, and way down there a gross little alley, and off to the left, some people and cars going about their lives."

Carrie smirks. "Yep."

"Yep? Yep what? It's not that interesting."

"What?" Carrie seems earnestly surprised. "You need to look closer, girl!"

Her expression is so genuine I look back out the window. I've been looking through this window in one way or another for months. All I see are the people that aren't trapped in here. I see lives being lived. I see everything I don't have.

I shake my head. "I'm sorry. I'm trying, but I really don't know what you mean."

Carrie groans. "Look there."

She points straight out the window.

"The office building?"

"Yes, the office building. Now look *into* the office building and tell me what you see."

Reluctantly, I hug my arms and walk closer to the glass, looking through the window, across the dank little alley, then through the window of the bustling office space across from us, not even twenty feet away. Both buildings are at least ten stories tall, though I have never bothered trying to count, and we are somewhere lost in the middle. The other building has allotted more ceiling height per floor than our little gray slab, so as the building gets higher, the floors are separating slightly from each other. Looking out the window I'm nearly even with an office space, but it's elevated just enough to make it feel like I'm looking up into a stage. I had never noticed that before. In fact, I've never really paid that much attention to the steel and glass across the alley because there didn't seem to be anything to pay attention to.

At first, I feel like I'm wasting my time. The workers are mostly at cubicle desks, and I can only see a handful of them between the windows and their gray piecemeal office walls. There's a middle-aged man with bushy, curly hair who looks uncomfortable in his skin. There's a younger guy in the cubicle next to him with headphones on, swaying back and forth while he types on his keyboard, clearly tuning out everything around him.

There's an empty cubicle that looks recently abandoned, with papers tacked to the walls around blank spaces that must have held photographs or mementos. There's a wall and then some sort of break room or kitchen with a few tables, a wall lined with cabinets, a sink, a fridge, and a vending machine. There are larger offices on either side of the bullpen and break room, but I can only see into a few of them, and only at a glancing angle.

"It's a normal office," I start to say when I see a young man carrying two full trays of coffee cups past the cubicle walls, headed towards the break room. He has a bag tucked under one arm and seems to be rushing. So much so that he trips upon entering the break room and, despite some mad scrambling, one of the coffees jiggles off the tray and falls spectacularly, hitting the ground lid first. As the lid pops off, the contents are flung out of the paper cup in a fantastic arc.

"Oh no!" I am captivated.

Coffee Man quickly collects himself and places the two trays with the other coffees on a table, looking over his shoulder and nudging the door closed with his foot. He sets the bag on the table with the coffees, picks up the dropped cup and spins it in his hand to read something scribbled on the side. Making a desperate, frustrated face he races to get paper towels. Once the coffee has been sopped up, he begins inspecting the other cups. Lifting the lid on one, he takes a whiff, shrugs, checks the name on the cup, and seems to take a moment to decide what to do. He looks back at the door briefly and then pours half of the contents of the full cup into the empty one, then tops off both cups from a sad-looking coffee maker in the corner. He then searches through the cabinet above the coffee maker and pulls out a couple bottles. He reads their labels, and with another shrug shakes a liberal amount of white powder from one of the containers into the cup that was spilled. He dries off the sides of the cup with a fresh paper towel and switches the sleeve with a clean one from another coffee cup.

Holding the Frankenstein coffee he straightens up, taking a deep breath. With an air of resolution, he opens the break room door and waves to

29

someone as he steps out into the hallway. I follow his path as he takes the coffee down the hall to one of the big offices that I can see. A woman with a smart suit and a severe bun looks up from her desk and motions to him. She looks at her watch and seems to say something to him while crossing her arms. Coffee Man sets down the cup and then nods his head a few times, keeping his arms tightly to his sides. She makes a dismissive gesture and he scurries out of the room.

I am amazed to realize I'm dying to see what she does when she drinks the concoction he's provided. But she sets the cup on her desk and I groan with frustration. After some typing, she takes the cup and leans back in her chair, spinning to look out the window. She takes a long, deep sip and chokes a bit

I burst out laughing. Carrie too, as she puts a hand on my shoulder. We collect ourselves to continue watching the show.

Manager Woman angrily slams down the coffee and shakes her hands. She must have spilled some coffee is trying to rid herself of the dripping liquid, pulling handfuls of Kleenex out of a box on her desk and dabbing at her shirt and skirt. She clearly yells towards her open door. A few of the cubicle workers turn around to see what the fuss is. Coffee Man is standing by Headphone's cubicle with a coffee in hand and leans over to talk to him. They appear deep in conversation, with Headphones removing his gear to listen, and looking towards Manager Woman's office and then back at Coffee Man. Coffee Man smirks proudly and they shudder with poorly contained wicked amusement. After a moment of this, Coffee Man gathers himself up and walks back to the window office, managing to appear shocked and gesturing to the cup.

Manager Woman picks up the cup and reviews the scribbles on its side, shaking her head and dismissing him again. As he walks past Headphones, the two surreptitiously high-five and Coffee Man continues to the break room, apparently to retrieve the remaining coffees.

"That was awesome," I admit.

Carrie is dabbing at little tears that have formed in the corners of her eyes. "Oh hell, that was better than I could've hoped for."

"So it isn't always this good?" I search the office building for more vignettes of entertainment.

"I wish it were, but probably not. We'll have to figure out their patterns. That's when it gets fun. Until then," she took a deep breath and headed away from the window, "we'll have to make some entertainment for ourselves."

She walks to one of the shelves with games on it and pulls out a Bicycle deck, one of the two that still has 52 cards, and returns to the table.

"That one uses a joker for the queen of hearts," I inform her as I sit across from her again.

"I know," she says, sounding slightly insulted. "I drew her in."

I always enjoyed the drawing of the queen of hearts in this deck. The Joker had been transformed by thick, black Sharpie into a stick figure queen, with angry eyebrows, a crooked crown, and a big, unwieldy scepter.

"I like her," I concede.

"I like her, too." She shuffles the deck and deals out ten cards to each of us.

- 6 -

KNOCKING

What started out as a contentious relationship has quickly turned into a solid friendship. Carrie, though often loud and rude, and definitely a cheater at cards, is a wonderful woman. Aside from our daily ritual of watching Office Building TV, usually in the morning and again at lunch, she has taught me gin rummy.

I initially thought it was just a way to pass the time in a stupor, but after she won her tenth consecutive game, I started trying to learn strategy. I've learned all about sequences and deadwood and knocking – all colorful terms that come along with gin rummy. The game is not that difficult to pick up, even with the more eccentric bit of physically knocking on the table as a way to indicate you want the hand to end, and thus be counted. The trouble isn't learning the game, but rather mastering it. I've found that it's half about playing your cards, and half about playing your opponent.

"Interesting," she comments after I discard the ace of diamonds. This is one of her many ways to screw with my head.

"Your Jedi mind tricks won't work on me, witch!" I hold up my cards like a shield in front of my face and peer over the edge with as much menace as I can muster while stifling a smile.

"I don't need mind tricks," she says calmly, while drawing a card from the deck.

"Interesting." I try to mimic the way she evaluates the decks. It makes her smirk, but in a way that makes me question if she is about to win again. I have a sequence of five cards in spades and a set of three sixes. I'm close to getting another sequence in low diamonds, and if I can just get the four, I'd finally have gin. I draw from the deck only to muffle a groan as the queen of diamonds is revealed.

Carrie cackles and reaches her hand out over the table.

"Don't you do it!" I threaten.

She hesitates for effect, like always, and then knocks.

"Gah!" I throw my head back in defeat again. I lay my cards on the table, knowing that queen just cost me an additional ten points when I could have knocked with the ace for one.

"I'd say you have a tell, kid, but your entire body is an open book." She chuckles under her breath while tallying the round. "That's a lot of deadwood," she grins again.

"Yeah, yeah." I shove the cards in her direction.

"Another win for me, so spill."

I sigh. This is the deal we made – if she wins, I have to talk about myself, and vice versa. At this point I know that her name is Carrie Griffin, and literally no other personal details.

"What would you like to know about this time?" I resign myself to another deep dive into my psyche.

"Why didn't you knock?"

"What?" She always asks me about my family, my childhood, my love life, my first kiss – all stuff I'd rather not discuss.

"Why didn't you knock when you had the ace? You would have gotten," she pauses to tally up the cards again, "one point."

I scowl at her.

"Well, it's not nothing!" she declares with a laugh.

"I was waiting for the inside straight."

"Sequence." She corrects me for the hundredth time.

"Yes, fine, sequence. I was waiting for the perfect hand to get gin, and I hadn't seen the four of diamonds, so I assumed it was still possible."

"You mean this four of diamonds?" She holds up one of her two deadwood cards.

"Yes, that one." I let my head fall into my hands and groan audibly.

"I think that's your trouble in life, kid."

"That I can't play cards to beat an old bat like you?"

She gives a hearty, throaty chuckle. "That, too, obviously. But I mean your *life* life, not your *card* life."

I look up at her. I have come to recognize that she has these little dollops of wisdom that I need to pay attention to. "Meaning?"

She nods. I think she likes it when she knows I'm preparing myself to listen to her. "I mean you don't appreciate what you have, but rather look to some sort of undefined possible future. You should take advantage of the opportunities that are presented to you. What is it about answering the door when opportunity – "

"Knocks." I cut her off with another scowl. "Very clever."

"I thought so," she chuckles with pride. "Seriously, though, you have a tough road here, I get that, but you can make something of it, somehow. Listen for the knock and stop waiting for the inside straight."

"Sequence," I correct her with a wicked grin. "Just deal." I lean back and wait.

"Not today, kid. I have an appointment, and so do you."

"What?" She never has appointments. At least, not that I can tell. We meet here in the mornings, have breakfast and chat. Dr. Strove apparently decided to bend some rules once Carrie explained her purpose here was to help me, and part of that was learning about each other over food. To be clear – all I know about her directly is her name, still, but I also know she likes some movies and music, though not ones I am familiar with.

Before I can ask her for more information, though, she is up and putting the cards away.

"Where are you going?" I sound more panicked than I intend, but I have a sort of separation anxiety after all that's happened. I cannot lose Carrie.

"Calm down," she says in a comforting voice. "I'll see you again for dinner." She doesn't explain what my appointment is or why she knows about it and I don't.

* * * *

I sit at the table for a little while. No "appointment" seems to be happening, so I decide to take a walk. I have gotten stronger over the last few weeks, so I'm more comfortable with wandering around the ward. It isn't large and there are still places I can't go, but there are a few spots that feel more hopeful to me now than they did before. There's a window that overlooks one of the busier freeways in the city. It's not pretty, but I like that it flows. It moves. It changes. Even if I'm stuck here, the world is still turning. Somehow, that makes me wonder if I still have a potential future. Something other than this, that is.

The other windows are in the game room and in some patient rooms not in the middle of the building like mine. I think they actually have to pay more for them, which I find strange since those patients are usually unconscious or here for a very short time.

The windows in the game room are still my favorite. Just like with the nurses in the ward, I have started naming the people that I regularly see on Office Building TV. (Carrie scolds me for not learning the nurses' actual names, but when I challenged her to tell me some, she couldn't manage it either. "You should make friends where you are," she says, "even if I'm too old to do it for myself.")

The office-building floor most closely planar to ours is the cubicle office, so we get the most fun out of them. It's a relatively diverse workforce, but nearly everyone seems miserable. Carrie and I have decided they are either in the medical industry, or something like car insurance. It doesn't matter, though. The only things that we really care about are the stories. The few times someone stands up from their cubicle, they look fairly downtrodden, so I'm also convinced there is a disparity in pay and benefits between the Cubies – my name for the cubicle workers – and the higher-ups in actual offices. There is Scruffy Cubie who always stands when Lady Cubie walks by. He lights up, and for one glorious moment, he seems happy – joyful even. Sometimes they talk, sometimes he just waves, but he always watches her until she's out of my line of sight, then he turns around with a heavy sigh and slumps his shoulders, sinking back below the height of the cubicle wall onto his chair.

There's Manager Lady, though she doesn't interact with the Cubies at all, as far as I can tell. Then we have Headphones, who doesn't seem to do much work at all, though he seems to be having a generally better time than some of the other workers. Coffee Man makes an occasional appearance to talk to Headphones, but it seems that he tries to avoid being near Manager Lady.

On the next floor up is the fun group. A different company, clearly, because they have bright walls, open tables, and no cubicle walls. I can't quite see into their floor because of the angle, but when they come close to the windows, they are usually smiling, sometimes tossing a ball back and forth, sometimes taping big sheets of paper to the window and standing around it, drawing and writing on the paper. And sometimes – my favorite times – they write straight onto the glass with what are apparently dry erase markers. That little bit that I can see makes me certain it's a tech company full of youth, vigor, and brilliance.

There are a lot of characters on the tech company floor, though I don't get to see them very often. There's Adonis, who earned his name because he's built, fashionable, and seems to be the head of everyone else.

Then there's Jasmine, who actually looks like the cartoon character from the Disney movie. She is gorgeous, with long, flowing black hair that she usually puts into a loose ponytail, and big, beautiful eyes that I can see even down here. Her eye makeup game is solid, as is her fashion sense.

There is Joy, a perky young woman who dresses in bright colors and seems to always be in a good mood.

And then there is my favorite, John. I call him John because he is so much of an everyman type of guy – in how he looks, dresses, his expressions – but he is also clearly sweet and everyone seems to like him. I would love to have a friend like Everyman John again; at least I think so, since I haven't had one of those for a while. Despite that, I like to think he and I would be best buds.

* * * *

A knock on the door brings me out of my reverie of voyeuristic storytelling. I know it's Carrie because she always knocks three times to get my attention, whereas everyone else just walks right in.

"Back so soon?" I say without looking away from the window. "Adonis is back at the window today, and I think Scruffy might actually ask Lady out on a date. Very exciting stuff."

"I'm sure."

I whip around. The man standing in the doorway is maybe a couple of years older than me, in a smart pair of jeans, ankle boots, a lavender button-down shirt, and a long white coat.

"I'm sorry," I stammer. "I thought you were someone else." I can feel my cheeks reddening.

"I assumed." He has a beautiful, rich accent that I can't place. He smiles. *What a smile.* His eyes pique up at the edges as he grins from ear to ear.

"Hi," he says.

My blood pressure cuff starts to beep slowly. *Son-of-a bitch.* I clamp my hand down over the sound in hopes that he won't be able to hear it.

37

"Hello," I say, a little too loudly, trying to muffle the sound of the monitor even more. It seems to make the cuff louder.

"Perhaps we should sit," he says, a bit of concern starting to spread into his features – the corners of his eyes turn down a little over his high cheekbones and the middle of his forehead pinches slightly underneath rich, tousled black curls.

Focus, focus, focus, I am screaming in my head.

"Of course," I agree in a horribly forced way. I make my way to the nearest table.

He walks over with both confidence and care, as though he's afraid I'll rabbit at the first opening. As he sits down smoothly across from me, I place my hands on the table, and then quickly cover the monitor again, to no avail. He identifies himself but I can't absorb it.

"May I?" He reaches towards me.

I extend my arm, thinking, *Is he going to kiss my hand?* The beeping picks up pace again.

Of course he doesn't kiss my hand, because that would be ridiculous, anachronistic, and completely inappropriate. Instead, he takes my wrist and looks to his watch to take my pulse. Right. He's a doctor. I think he said so. Hence the white coat and his improbable presence in this place.

The beeping slows down as my senses return to me. He seems appeased with this and with my pulse and releases my wrist.

"You're probably wondering who I am and why I'm here." His features relax and the corners of his mouth turn up slightly.

"Just a little." I smile in response. Like, *really* smile. My cheeks start hurting a little as I haven't stretched my lips this much or this broadly in a long time.

"Right. Again, I'm Dr. Ghazanfer Choudhury."

"Nice to meet you, Dr. Chowder-hurry." I know I butchered it and I grimace a little.

"Choudhury, but don't worry. Just call me Riaz."

"Riaz. I can manage that," I say with pinking cheeks. "I don't want to insult you, though. I could also learn your full name. I'm sorry I butchered it."

He looks contemplative for a second. "Thank you. I appreciate that. But, everyone calls me Riaz. It's no insult. And Dr. Choudhury can become a bit of a tongue twister. Besides, it is important to me that we can have easy conversation."

"Sure." I realize too late that I have tilted my head to the side and sighed like a lovesick schoolgirl. I straighten up in my chair. "You can call me Taylor." I clear my throat. "So how can I help you, Dr. Riaz?"

"Just Riaz." He smiles again, and damn if it's not the best smile. "And actually, I am here to help you, Taylor."

"Great!" I'm trying to temper my excitement. "I mean, I don't meet a lot of new people."

"Except for Adonis and Scruffy?" He laughs.

This elicits a genuine reaction from me and I can feel some of my tension lessen.

"Yes, well, I've known them for over a week, now. They don't count. You, however, are a mystery."

"Well, that won't do." He leans back in his chair. "Let's see, I was born in Pakistan, moved to London for school, and started working in a research facility after getting my doctorate. Since then I have been studying brains."

I'm stunned and quiet for a second. He raises his eyebrows. I blink away my initial shock and nod. "I think I just learned more about you in ten seconds than I know about any other single person in this place. So, thanks for that!"

"You're welcome?" He looks at me with a questioning stare.

"But, that only gets you so far," I chide playfully. "Brains are a pretty complex subject, or so I'm told. That's a pretty broad field of study."

He takes a breath. Something in his hesitation makes me realize his expertise is going to be bad news for me.

"Ah," I say before he can continue. "That bad, huh?"

"Not bad," he hurries to correct. "Just… complicated. I specialize in brain conditions and injuries that cause hallucinations."

"Okay then." I sit back into my chair a little heavily. "So we're certain they are hallucinations, now?"

Riaz sits back, mirroring my posture. "I think we don't really know much of anything. You're the real mystery." He raises one eyebrow in a shockingly and unintentionally sexy way.

Oh man, I'm screwed.

- 7 -

SESSIONS

Riaz has been to the facility nearly every day since we met three days ago, checking in with a brief hello before heading to Dr. Strove's office. Even though I don't normally know what day of the week it is, I have started to take an interest in calendars and clocks again, aware that Riaz will probably not work on weekends.

He has been going over my charts and data in Strove's office, which is on the other side of the building from the game room and other places that I normally go. So I've been walking the halls hoping to get a glimpse of him as well as catch a phrase or two about my status – or, at least, what Riaz thinks of my status.

But other than the occasional instances of "accidentally" bumping into him, the embarrassment of which is metered only slightly by the dimples I glimpse as he lights up before he walks around me, I've been generally unsuccessful.

So I don't know much. I do know, however, that my "sessions," as he called them, with Riaz start today. Today at noon.

* * * *

"Stop fidgeting, it's not even ten yet." Carrie pulls another card from the gin rummy stockpile.

"Right, sorry." I try to focus back on the cards and discard an eight of clubs.

She scowls. "You're not paying attention. You shouldn't toss that eight."

I look in my hand. "But I don't need it." I have a sequence in spades from eight to jack, and I have started sets of threes and aces.

"You have another eight, and judging from the current discards, both eights are still available. I think you might even have another eight in your deadwood."

She was right. I had hidden it accidentally with the other cards.

"But my other eight is in a sequence, so I only have one."

"You can share cards between melds." She throws her cards down. "This is pointless."

She leans back and crosses her arms.

"Sorry." I apologize earnestly, setting my cards down.

"That's okay, I was going to win again anyway."

I sigh. "I don't doubt it."

"You look worried. What are you worried about?"

"I'm not worried, just, you know, totally freaked out."

"Which is different how?"

"No, you're right, I'm worried. I'm worried he'll see me as a lab rat instead of a person. I'm worried he won't be able to figure out what's wrong with me. I'm worried he will." My voice trails off.

"Worried he will? So if he figures it out and, what, can't treat it?"

"Yes," I agree. "And/or can treat it but the treatment's worse than the disease. Or treats it perfectly and I'm released with nothing."

"Wow. There is a lot to unpack there." She leans forward on her elbows, cradling her chin in a way that has become quite endearing. I mirror her so we aren't more than two feet apart.

"What do I do, Carrie? I can't stay here forever, but I also have nothing left to go to. There is nothing out there for me."

Carrie shakes her head. I've already told her my sad story, so she knows I'm not being entirely dramatic. She shrugs. "All of that is good stuff to worry about, but you shouldn't start worrying prematurely. Let the kid work."

"Doctor," I correct her.

She smiles. "You're all kids to me. Now deal us a fresh hand."

* * * *

I'm in my room ten minutes early. That ten minutes is long, waiting for Riaz and the beginning of the next phase, whatever that means. Riaz is precisely on time. I find that charming. I hate being late, and appreciate people who are on time.

He walks in and looks around briefly. "There aren't any chairs," he says mostly to himself.

"I'm not allowed to have lots of things," I shrug. "Punishment."

He seems bothered by this. "That's rubbish, but no worries. Let's go to the game room."

* * * *

I had assumed "sessions" meant more tests and blood draws and monitors. But Riaz has no medical equipment, just a thick file, a black Pilot G-2 pen, and a yellow legal pad.

He places all of his paperwork on the table and laces his fingers over the top of the mound, leaning on his elbows. "You a bit nervous?"

I stare at him blankly. I must look like a deer in headlights.

"If it eases your mind," he says, "I am always a bit nervous at this stage, too. Do you think you're ready anyway?"

"I guess?" I acknowledge this with a slow shrug.

"Not a thoroughly confident answer, but I'll take that as a yes." He removes a heap of papers from the file, tapping the stack on the table to make it meticulously even and straight. It's exactly what I would do. I relax a little and he seems to as well.

"Okay, so we are going to determine what is going on with you and figure out how to manage it, sound alright?"

"Sounds great," I lie.

"Brilliant." His accent comes out a little thick, but he doesn't seem to notice.

The edges of my lips begin to curve upwards, but suddenly the unknown future holds more terror for me than this mundane but familiar life. As long as I have Carrie, Office Building TV, Riaz and Strove, I feel I can manage this. But *out there*, what would I do?

"Dr. Strove has been thorough." Riaz motions to the huge file on the table and the collection of papers in his hands. "But I want to go back over some of his conclusions and data to see if I can discern any patterns that he isn't seeing, or try and more specifically identify the types of hallucinations, or other conditions, that are happening during your lapses."

He flips through some pages, his lips moving silently as he counts something within the files. "I see here you've had eleven of these episodes to date?" He looks at me for confirmation.

"If that's what it says." I shrug.

"We need to get this under control right away, then! So, in the interest of time," he continues, "I am just going to get right to it. Tell me, in your own words, what happened when your symptoms began."

I take a deep breath and sigh. "Well, let's see. My sister was killed in a car accident and I woke up in the hospital. Since then, I've gone insane."

Riaz looks up from his page, his pen poised above the empty lines, clearly waiting to write down something more than what I just said. He puts the pen down. "I didn't realize your sister was in the car with you."

I hardly ever think about her anymore, because when I do, I break down. The complicated mixture of pain and grief from the actual loss, and the guilt and shame about everything that happened before and since can easily overwhelm me. "Yeah," is all I can manage to whisper. The lump that has taken up permanent residence in my throat begins to swell.

I can hear the beeping on the monitor, but I am far away, stuck in my thoughts, drowning in the hurricane of my anguish. It's times like these that the lapses seem to happen. Times when I am vulnerable or emotional. I'm certain one is going to start soon, so I lay my head onto my hands to avoid another head injury if I should have a seizure. I can sense the darkness coming when I feel a soft warmth on my clasped fists. It brings me back. It is Riaz, holding my hands in his. I look up and he is staring right into my eyes. He pulls me back like an anchor line snaps and halts a drifting boat.

"I'm so sorry to hear that," he gently pats my hands. "I cannot imagine the weight of that loss." He seems to consider his options carefully, evaluating me as he does. He runs a hand through his hair, having apparently come to a decision.

"My sister and I are eleven years apart," he says, "so I never really bonded with her in the same way you must have with your sister, but I would be lost without her."

I blink, not quite sure what he is doing.

"She's a funny girl, Liyana. She's skinny as a stick and a tomboy to boot. My poor mother wishes she were a delicate flower who will someday marry a respectable Pakistani man, but she is a handful. The name Liyana actually means tender woman, which couldn't be further from the truth." He talks with his hands, crossing them in front of him to emphasize just how far from a tender woman his sister is.

"Brilliant and kind, don't get me wrong," he explains, "but tender? No bloody way!"

He continues telling me about his sister, his parents, and his home growing up in Pakistan. He makes me laugh, allows me to bite my cheek and choke down some tears, and doesn't call attention to my emotions or sniffles. He simultaneously grounds me and distracts me so that I can work through my pain in the company of someone who isn't demanding my attention or trying to manage me.

It's one of the greatest gifts anyone has ever given me, and I love him for it.

- 8 -

THE FIRST LAPSE

Riaz didn't ask more of me that day, but I knew, and he knew, we would have to get to the actual trauma before any real progress could be made. We had agreed to meet in the game room again, and the next day Carrie slips out half an hour before he arrives. I pass the time with some Office Building TV.

When he enters the room I give a nervous wave and he returns it with a comforting, though knowing, wave of his own.

"Shall we get started?" he asks, motioning to a chair at the table. It's a real question, not just a command. It was as if he were asking me if I was ready and able to tackle this.

I'm not. I will never be. But I am going to do it anyway. I manage a nod and take my seat.

"Okay," he starts gently. "Tell me about what led up to the accident."

I feel my eyes go wide as I shake my head. "Instead of that, which is a really long and horrible story, let me tell you about waking up in the hospital."

Riaz gestures agreeably with his hand. "If you think that's best."

I take a deep breath.

"I woke up in pain. My arm was broken, I had bruised ribs, a herniated disc, a broken ankle, whiplash, and, of course, the head trauma. I remembered that I had been driving, though at first I couldn't remember why. I didn't remember that Syd, Sydney, my sister, was in the car. The cast on my arm, brace on my ankle, and all the bandages felt very constricting, like I was being held hostage. That created a panic that led to me flailing around, trying to get out of the bed, out of the wires and bandages. The nurses rushed in, all consoling and sweetness. I can see their faces now and I know what they must have been thinking, but then I just was afraid. That's when the first lapse happened.

"I went from being in the hospital bed to suddenly, in this horrible blur, standing at the open bar at my sister's wedding. The panic was still there, and now confusion as well, but I was certain it was not a dream. It was real. I could feel the straps at my heels digging into my ankles, but the pain of the broken ankle was gone. I held my arms out in front of me to check for any casts, and discovered I was free of bandages and restraints. At that moment, looking down at myself and feeling perfectly fine, it felt more like the hospital had been a bad dream or some sort of hallucination or panic attack. There was no evidence that the hospital was real. I pressed gently on my ribs, felt my head, and then shook it all off like I was crazy, because that was the only explanation.

"On the other hand, I knew I had already been to the wedding, that it had already happened, but I also felt like maybe everything that had happened since the wedding was a weird, horrible, realistic nightmare. Or maybe it was all an absence seizure that happened in the blink of an eye and I felt like I lived those years, but it was a trick of my mind. Maybe I really was at the wedding again. Or, I guess, still at the wedding. But there was too much that I already knew was going to happen. Things that I could sense before they started. Things I couldn't possibly know.

"For instance, our childhood friend approached me and we talked about her kid, but I knew what she was going to say. My uncle told a bad joke but before I turned around to look at him, I knew our friends had good-naturedly feigned amusement for his benefit and then meandered away. Things like that. But I wasn't just remembering them, I was reliving them.

"I felt a pull to go through the motions, you know? Like I still had to do everything the same. Like the script was still there and I had to play along or the whole scene would screw up. I went to the room where my sister was getting ready, helped her with her veil and her ring and led her out to the aisle. All of it was as it had been on that day, but real, not memory. I can't explain it well enough, but it was real. *Real* real. I stumbled over a cobblestone, I was perspiring in the heat of the day and I could feel the sweat running down my armpit. I watched the proceedings, looked around the crowd, looked at *him*. I was having real thoughts, real misgivings about the whole situation, real anger, but also remembering that this had all happened before.

"The next thing I knew, there was another horrific blur and I was back in the hospital room. I was surrounded by even more nurses and doctors. There were beeping machines, a tube down my throat, my gown was lying open, which was not the best feeling, and there were these patches on my chest.

"And then the pain came back, almost slowly, as if it had to catch up to me. But soon it was excruciating, and there were new pains and discomforts, like the tube down my throat, and I was reeling. Reeling from the relived wedding day, from the pain, from confusion, and actual fear. I was terrified. But they weren't concerned with my mind at that point, just my body.

"Apparently, I had been seizing, hypotensive, my heart rate was irregular, and a whole slew of other things I don't remember." I shake my head.

Riaz flips through the file, making notes on the legal pad. He scratches little check marks on different parts of the file and raises his eyebrows. "Yes, a whole slew of other things," he says, mostly to himself.

Amused, I relax a little more. "Anyway, I was under observation in the ICU for three or four days, then in a regular ward for another week. During that time I had MRIs and CT scans and x-rays and ultrasounds, and all the things that you can do to look inside someone. Except surgery," I correct quickly, "because that would have been weird."

Riaz chuckles. "I have to agree. There would have been no need for laparoscopy. It is good to have these images, though I wish we had a baseline." He holds various films up to the window light and squints to see the information more clearly. He catches himself and taps the scans on the table to straighten them and puts the pile off to the side. "I'm sorry, please continue."

"Actually, that's pretty much it. That was the beginning of this ride."

Riaz shakes his head with astonishment. "Okay, so some clarification." He flips to the front page of his notes. "You had your first lapse after being in the hospital for how many days?"

"I think they told me I had been out for two days before I woke up."

"Okay, and do you think you had the lapse because of your stress level?"

I shrug. "Stress, panic, anxiety, confusion. There were lots of great emotions. One thing for sure, though, is that there were emotions, if you see what I mean."

Riaz studies the file and his notes with pursed lips. "So the lapses seem to be triggered by neurotransmitters or hormones related to strong emotions."

"Sure," I agree without knowing what else to say.

Riaz looks up at me and puts the notepad down with an embarrassed grimace. "Sorry, just trying to start thinking about the possibilities. Was that a part of your accident, then?" He points with his pen to my burn scar.

"No," I answer quickly, covering it subconsciously with my right hand.

"Oh," he says in a knowing way, as his eyes dart to the bandage on my right arm.

"No!" I correct him. "I didn't do this to myself. It's from an accident when I was young."

"I see," he says, still eyeing my right arm.

"Yeah, this is my first time in the Rookery!" I say a bit too enthusiastically, waving my bandaged arm as evidence.

He looks confused. "Sorry?"

"Oh, you know, because 'I'm a raven'…" I want to slam my face into my hands and hide under the table. I feel my cheeks pinking. I quickly add, "It's from a book I love. Just a concept."

"What book?" he says, a look of recognition passing over his face.

"Oh, it's a book called *The Name of the Wind*, this sort of epic fantasy novel."

"Oh my gosh, I love that book! Have you read the other one?" His enthusiasm is infectious.

"Of course! How can you stop without knowing what happens? Well, I mean, until you run out of books."

"Oh, I know!" He throws his hands up and shakes his head. "I cannot believe we don't even have a release date for *The Doors of Stone*."

"Wow, I didn't even know what it was called. It's just been 'the elusive Book Three' to me," I giggle. This is a real conversation about something we have in common. He's a fan of at least one thing I'm a fan of. It's a connection, a *real* connection. And that is probably why Riaz looks taken aback and clears his throat. He runs his hand through his hair again. I think it may be a nervous tick. It's like he is putting a mask back on. I wish I hadn't said anything, just let the moment continue.

"Sorry," he starts, but I cut him off.

"No! No need! I love talking about books."

"Right," he says with a look of guilt. "We should probably stick to the medical stuff, though."

And just like that, the moment is gone. The connection feels severed in its infancy. I can feel my whole body fall. More than that, I can feel something in me that had been lifted up falling, too. That bit of camaraderie or connection just sinking to the pit of my stomach.

"So," he continues without ceremony. "When did the second lapse happen?"

I feel as though I can barely breathe. I look him right in the eye. "When they told me what happened to Sydney."

- 9 -

WAR AND CUBIES

Our meeting was cut short after my blood pressure went up again and the nurses started to attend to me with a little more concern. When they entered the room, Riaz nodded and stood, writing down the information that they were spouting off, like my pulse rate, blood pressure, and temperature. I was sitting through the whole process like a limp doll. If someone had wanted to practice how to do basic intake procedures, I would have been the perfect candidate.

I did catch Riaz looking at me with something other than clinical interest or guilt. It was like he was evaluating me in a different way, evaluating something other than my medical condition, though it was unclear what that might be. After the nurses were satisfied that I wasn't going to lapse or burst into some kind of dangerous fit, they walked off together, chatting about some reality TV show they were all obsessed with. I almost asked if they ever watched Office Building TV, but I didn't have the energy to deal with their stares or pity.

Riaz took the opportunity of their leaving to follow behind the nurses, waving at me half-heartedly and mentioning something about picking up where we left off tomorrow. And then I was all alone again.

It takes a minute or two for me to get out of my own head. If Riaz isn't in the room, there's no need for me to keep dwelling on the past that I couldn't change with my sister, or the future that's clearly not going to happen with Riaz. I'm back to my lonely self, trying to figure out some sort of next move to make my life a little more livable.

I spin my chair around and move it closer to the window, propping my feet up on the metal bar of the windowsill. It is just past lunchtime, so the office workers are getting back to their desks, tossing out their fast-food wrappers or empty brown lunch bags.

Scruffy Cubie is hastily finishing up what looks like a homemade salad, stuffing the empty Tupperware into a drawer, cleaning off his face with a napkin and looking over his shoulder. Though I can't see them, I assume that some of his coworkers have just returned via the elevator.

Sure enough, a minute later Manager Woman heads to her office with her afternoon fancy coffee – she's stopped asking Coffee Man to get her coffee as far as I can tell, though he still does so for the rest of the office. She rolls her executive chair up to her desk and starts checking emails or doing whatever it is she does. Beyond her office I can see another gaggle of people walking towards the cubicles. I always hope a little that one of them will be Lady Cubie, because Scruffy lights up when she walks by.

He clearly wishes it, too, as he cranes his neck as surreptitiously as he can, which is to say not at all, and his shoulders slump a little when she doesn't pass by.

"Give it time, Scruffy."

"Give what time?" Carrie walks up behind me, her mouth full of something. "Sorry, I just got these." She hands me a turkey sandwich and pulls up her own chair, placing her feet on the metal bar next to mine.

"Lady Cubie isn't back from lunch, yet."

Carrie nods, finishing her mouthful before responding. "He really is smitten, isn't he?"

"Totally head over heels, I imagine. But she doesn't give him the time of day. She's polite, to be sure, but dismissive and distant. She deserves better."

"She? Are we still talking about Scruffy or are we talking about Lady?" She looks me over. "Or are we talking about someone else entirely?"

I blush a little but try to ignore it. "He, I obviously meant he. He deserves better. Deserves to be treated with kindness and respect."

Carrie slowly rocks back and forth on her chair, its front legs come up off the ground a little as she does so. "What makes you think he, sorry, she, doesn't respect... him?" She looks as though she's getting tripped up in what she's saying versus what she's thinking.

"She," I emphasize strongly. "Doesn't ever stop to talk to him. She just waves and walks by, even though he is clearly straining to greet her. And, yeah, sure he's not the most handsome guy and he could use a fashion lesson or two, but he's a hard worker and he is attentive and smart."

"Uh huh." Carrie is just staring at me now. "And you can tell all of this at sixty feet in the air, across the alley, through the window?"

I slump. "I think it's that way. That's the story of Scruffy and Lady. The story that keeps me coming back day after day for the next installment."

Carrie returns her attention to the office building. She takes a big bite out of her sandwich and we sit in silence for a few minutes.

When Lady does come back to the office, we are almost as excited as Scruffy. He stands up and nervously waves to her as she passes. We both faux cheer when we see her, but then we nearly gasp when she stops, turns towards him, laughs a little at something he said, shrugs shyly and walks away from him, tucking a bit of hair behind her ear as she goes, sneaking a final glance at him before she is out of sight.

We leap out of our chairs. Carrie is waving her hands around and bits of her sandwich are falling off in every direction.

I jump up and down a little, a huge grin spreading across my face. "I'm so glad for him! They talked – did you see that? She smiled!"

"Mmm hmmm," she manages through closed lips, still chewing her big bite.

I know that it's a strange thing to get so excited about this small encounter. Especially considering we don't actually know what's happening between the two of them. But it doesn't matter. The fact of the situation is greatly outweighed by the fiction that we created. The fiction that we need. That I need.

After a bit we calm ourselves and sit back down. I suddenly have an appetite and take the plastic wrap off of the sandwich Carrie brought me and take a bite. I look over at her.

"I know," she says, shaking her head, "I didn't forget. They were out of mustard packets."

"Another luxury lost," I sigh.

"So." Carrie situates herself back onto her chair and props her feet back up. "Are we going to talk about what's really going on?"

"No," I growl to her, knowing that she will get it out of me one way or another.

She looks me over for a second. "Do I have to beat your skinny butt at gin rummy again?"

"Not that I don't love it when you hand my ass to me, but I don't want to talk about it."

Carrie finishes her sandwich in one big bite and stands, holding her hand out for my plastic wrap. She takes the trash to the trashcan and grabs the deck of cards on her way back.

"Noooooo," I groan.

"Not gin, just war."

"War?" I ask. "Like when you flip a card over and if yours is higher you win the battle?"

"Yep."

"Okay." I turn towards her, my interest piqued. "But if I win a battle, you have to talk, too."

She eyes me suspiciously. "Whoever wins three in a row asks the question, loser talks."

"Deal." We drag our chairs over to the table and sit across from each other.

The first three she wins. Carrie grins. "What's on your mind?"

"That you're cheating with a stacked deck."

She chortles and we draw the next bunch.

She wins the first one, I win the next two, then one for her, three for me.

"Ha!" I've never won before. This is so exciting! My mind is racing for a good question.

"How do you know Dr. Strove?" I ask triumphantly.

"I used to be his patient. Wasted question, you already knew that."

She's right. I could slap myself.

The next question goes to me, again. "Why are you friends with Dr. Strove? Because just being his patient doesn't mean friendship, obviously!"

She chews on her bottom lip thoughtfully. "Smart girl." She pauses, looking down at the cards and absentmindedly stroking the gold chain around her neck. I suddenly remember how jealous I was that she got to wear something like that and feel ashamed.

"He was also my husband's doctor, before I ever had issues. And we spent a lot of time together trying to make Norman's life better. The Doc and I just bonded, I guess."

"What happened to him, your husband?" I ask gently, she's never even mentioned that she had a husband.

"Nope! You have to beat me again for another question, girly." She quickly jerks her hand away from the necklace and returns to her normal posture.

We go on like this for an hour. I find out that her husband died young of some terrible neurological disease that I can't pronounce. She and Strove had become friends over the course of her husband's treatment and then, when she had her own seizures, years later, they were still friends and he arranged to bring her on as a patient of the clinic, though he made sure she was treated by another doctor. Our Dr. Strove would never break the rules, not even for an actual friend.

She learns that I have never been able to make friends easily, and in fact don't have any outside of these walls at this point. But she finally gets to what she really wants; I admit to her that I'm disappointed in how Riaz had opened up about books and then shut me down soon after. I tell her it's the first connection I have had besides my friendship with her and it seemed cruel not to allow it. I'm a little nervous about how she'll react.

She slams a queen down over my jack. "Ha! So what are you going to do about it?"

I shrug, resigned. "What can I do? He wants to keep it professional, which I guess is the right thing to do, but I don't want to talk to him about all this personal stuff and just be a lab rat, you know?"

She nods. "Right, so you're going to tell him that." It was not a question.

"What?" I shake my head.

"Tell him everything you just said to me, only maybe leave out the part where you have a crush on him."

"I never said that!" I blush again. "Why would you say that?"

"I'll answer this one for free, kiddo. You can read it all over your face when he walks in the room."

- 10 -

SECOND CHANCES

Over the next couple of days, Carrie's comments race through my mind. Not just about how I'm apparently transparent when it comes to my attraction to Riaz, but also that I should tell him how I feel. I want to believe she is right, but at the same time, I enjoy my sessions with Riaz and I don't want to scare him away. It's been a few days since he has been around – I think it's the weekend maybe – and I've been trying to figure out what to do.

Of course, if he isn't going to be open with me, maybe time with him wouldn't be so interesting after all.

At breakfast, Carrie and I both push powdered eggs around our cheap plastic plates. I shove mine away in favor of buttered toast. I look up at her, but before I can say anything, she interjects.

"I know, I know. There was no jelly today. Only marmalade and I know you hate that stuff."

"This is getting ridiculous. First no mustard, now no jelly. Are we prisoners or patients?"

"Is there a difference?" Carrie picks up her dry-looking English muffin and tears a piece off the edge, eating it thoughtfully. "Are you going to talk to him?"

I sigh. "I really don't know. I can't decide. He's a nice guy, maybe he would understand. But maybe it would be better for all of us if the whole thing were just patient-doctor with no friendliness."

"I promise you it won't be better for all of us."

I eye her suspiciously.

"Because it won't be better for me if you sulk around all day and don't concentrate on cards."

I can't help but laugh. "You know what?" I put my hands squarely on the tabletop. "I am going to do it."

"Do what?" comes Riaz's unmistakable voice.

"None of your beeswax, Doc." Carrie stands with her back to him and winks at me. Then she takes both our plates and heads out of the room.

"Um, alright," Riaz says, nervously looking over his shoulder at where she has gone.

"Don't take it personally. It's her way of saying she doesn't care what anyone thinks of her and damn it all if she's going to give away any personal details."

"Yeah, she seems like quite the character."

"She is. And she's amazing," I say earnestly and I appreciate Carrie for a moment. She warms my heart.

"So, what's new?" he asks cheerily.

"Same ol', same ol'," I say, scowling a bit.

"Right, of course." He shakes his head. "I wasn't thinking. Just a habit, I guess."

He sits across from me. "Before we start – " he begins.

"Wait, actually, I'm sorry to interrupt, but I just think I need to say something first. If that's okay." I stutter it out in an incoherent mess, but he seems to get my gist. I clear my throat. "Look, I get that I'm your patient, and I know that you have to be professional and all, and I'm all for it, of course, but I'm also not a lab rat. You need to understand that I have been in here without anyone but Carrie to talk to for months. I don't really know how many, which now that I'm thinking about it is kind of a terrifying realization."

Riaz's eyebrows arch up and he stares at me with a look of confusion and amusement.

"Sorry, I'm carrying on, um, what I was trying to say, I mean, what I need to say, is that I am done being an experiment. I mean, I am a person. Like, a real, live person with feelings and thoughts and opinions. And no friends."

"Except for Ms. Griffin," he corrects.

"Of course, except her. But I've never been able to make friends easily. Before her, there were months of no friends here, just Dr. Strove being aloof and nurses going through this place like it's a discount store on Black Friday."

"I see." He's smiling slightly now. "And so what is it that you are asking?"

I feel myself blushing, which makes me blush even more. My cheeks are tangibly heating up. "Just that I will answer your questions so long as you are willing to have an actual conversation."

"Alright," he says, clearly trying to prevent a grin from reaching the corners of his mouth.

"Because all of this really personal stuff may or may not actually help you determine what is wrong with my brain. So why should I tell you unless there is some kind of camaraderie, like you and I can have a relationship…" I almost choke on the word. "I mean, like, a friendship. We should be able to have a friendship."

"Alright," he says again, smiling even more now.

"Okay." I take a deep breath and relax a little. "What was it that you wanted to say?"

"I was going to say that I think we should make these sessions a little less rigorous and more conversational."

"Oh." I grimace. "I should have let you go first."

"That wouldn't have been nearly as much fun." He chuckles slightly under his breath. "For me, of course."

"Yeah, yeah, yeah." I shake my head to try and dissipate my embarrassment.

"Alright, so before we start …" he repeats, giving me a look that says he's testing the water to see if I'll interrupt again.

"Please proceed," I direct him in my most formal-sounding voice.

His face softens and he takes a deep breath. "So how can I make you feel more at ease?"

I hadn't thought about it. I didn't even think I would get this far, so the offer was a little out of left field for me. "Um, what's your favorite movie?"

He shakes his head. "That is a ridiculous question."

"What? Why? Don't you like movies?" I scrutinize his face.

"Of course I do. I love them. Which is why trying to pick a single one would be nearly impossible. Even picking one per genre would be difficult at best. Could you pick a favorite if I asked you?"

"You have a point," I concede. "Okay, then, what's the last movie you saw and what were your impressions?"

"This last weekend I saw a re-run of a classic, actually."

"Intriguing." I cross my arms. "Well? What was it?"

"Don't laugh, it's actually a really wonderful film, and when I saw that it was playing in a theater, I couldn't resist. I've never seen it in a theater before."

"My mind is coming up with non-flattering options, so you better just come clean."

"I saw *The Princess Bride* at a little theater not far from my place."

My jaw drops a little. "That is one of my all-time favorite movies! What theater was it playing at?"

"A little independent theater called La Paloma?" He says it as if it were a question, like he isn't sure that's what it was called.

"That is the best theater! How have you never been there before, especially if it's near your house?"

"Hotel," he corrects, "and to be fair, I have only been in town for a couple of weeks."

"Hotel? I'm so sorry. I didn't know."

"Nothing to apologize for. I found your case intriguing enough to take a semester off from teaching so that I could figure you out. As best as anyone could figure you out." He smiles a little. "But it's a lovely area, so I am not complaining."

I had no idea he traveled to see me. I try to redirect the conversation. "I can't believe I missed it!" I put my hands over my face and lean back, faux wailing to the ceiling.

"I am sorry you missed it. The theater was brilliant and seeing it on the big screen was fantastic. The only trouble was, and you're going to think I'm an idiot, but I forgot what day it was."

I look back to him. "I don't really even know what month it is. I just don't keep track of that stuff anymore. What day was it?"

He clears his throat a little, seemingly embarrassed. "It was Valentine's Day."

Awkward. I could have figured it out if I would have taken a second to think about it. I try to push on. "Yikes. What kind of trouble are we talking about? First date on Valentine's Day? Forgot to buy that special someone some flowers? You went in your lab coat?"

He chuckles uncomfortably. "No. No date or special someone or lab coat. Just the only chap there by himself. The only empty seat in the place was right next to me. It was quite mortifying."

"That's rough."

"It was fairly uncomfortable until the film started and I just got swept away. Luckily, everyone else was there for the story as well, so there wasn't any snogging or funny business."

"Snogging or funny business?" I bite my lips together, eyes wide with delight.

"What? You know what I mean! How bizarre would it have been if everyone else was canoodling during the whole movie? That would have made it abso-bloody-lutely the worst."

"Agreed." I stifle a laugh. "Glad there was no bloody funny business or canoodling," I say, using my best British accent.

"Ha ha," he says dryly. "Your turn." He thinks for a second, tapping his pen on his lips as he looks up at the ceiling, like he's going to snatch inspiration from the stained, cracked ceiling panels. "Ah! What is *one of*," he stresses the words, "your favorite books? And it can't be *The Name of the Wind* because we already covered that."

"Oh, okay." It's my turn to think. "There are a lot, but the first three that come to mind are *Life of Pi*, *The Education of Little Tree*, and *A Man Called Ove*."

He nods thoughtfully. "Okay, then. Now I know that you have difficulty following simple directions…" He mimics writing something down on his legal pad.

"Hey!" I protest.

"I would love to hear more about your sister, from before. I told you all about Liyana and my mother and father. It could be a good way to get to know you better."

"Yeah." I become nostalgic, thinking of Sydney before Chris. "I haven't really thought about that, about her before… well, in a while. Could be nice."

We spend the next hour just talking. He finds it particularly amusing that Sydney and I used to boy watch, prying to find out what type of guys we were into at thirteen and sixteen. My descriptions of some of the more memorable candidates get a huge laugh and he admits he was a bit of a nerd for the first half of secondary school, which he explains was his high school experience. It's my turn to enjoy his vivid descriptions of his braces and baggie jeans. He admits he was trying to fit in with the skater crowd in his London neighborhood, but he was too afraid to attempt tricks for fear of damaging his head.

"So you've always been a brain guy?" I am still giggling from the picture in my head of a smaller, crooked-toothed Riaz carrying his skateboard all over town to try and fit in.

"I suppose I have," he admits. "It seemed such a shame to damage one's mind. Even with the helmet and all the pads, I was terrified."

"I can just picture little Riaz running around trying to keep up with his friends."

"Lucky for me, I found some better mates who were into the same things I was into."

"Such as?" I lean in with anticipation.

"Such as puzzles," he admits.

"Puzzles. Like, thousand-piece tabletop pictures of cats and dogs?"

"No," he says, feigning defensiveness. "Like Rubik's Cubes. Things that need to be solved, not just things that are out of order."

He sees the questioning look on my face and sighs. "I realize they are both things that are out of order, but I mean the types of things that can be solved in lots of ways. There is no single path to a solution."

"I see." I study his face with new appreciation for his depth and mystery. "So, puzzles and skaters. Is that all?"

"No," he says. "I found mates who were into the same types of books and films as me and, eventually, girls." He winks and grins.

"Had lots of girlfriends, huh?"

He guffaws. "No, I did not. We were more observers than participants. Half the time it was like we were on safari, trying to understand lions."

"Lionesses," I correct with a nudge.

"So true!"

"I bet all the girls like you."

"All evidence to the contrary." He clears his throat and sits up a little in his chair.

"We've been talking for an hour," I note. I'm impressed at how easily we converse. "Should we get on with it?"

"Very well, then." He squares up to me and poises his pen over his legal pad, for real this time. "Shall we try this medical thing again?"

- 11 -

CRUSHED

I settle in for another bout of storytelling, tucking my legs up onto the chair and leaning back. Riaz is waiting patiently but also has an expectant look on his face like he is actually interested in the story rather than just the science. I don't know why, but that makes me a little lightheaded.

But the show must go on.

"Okay," I start with a big sigh. "The first episode, or lapse, or fit, or whatever you want to call it, was explained away by the doctors as a traumatic hallucination due to the accident. After a few days of close observation, I was going to be released and they were gathering my things – the earrings and ring I had been wearing in the wreck, the boot that they didn't cut off my ankle, my bag and wallet, and my phone." It's harder to recount than I expected, but I press on. "I had asked them earlier if I had any visitors and they said that the ICU is off limits to visitors. So much was going on I didn't really think about it. When they handed me my phone, my first thought was how much the spiderweb crack was going to cost me to fix, but then I saw it was also dented. When I turned it on, the screen was fritzing. It still worked, the nurse told me, so they didn't know what to do with it. I carefully flicked the screen up and found that I had about twenty texts from my friend Aaron, but nothing from anyone else. I flicked to the first of Aaron's texts and he said something about being so sorry about Sydney.

"It didn't register. Then I remembered, in a blinding flash, that she had been in the car. I remembered the headlights, just like in the movies, but then nothing – no car spinning in slow motion with shattered glass spraying up all around us. Then I got it. My jaw dropped. I asked them if my sister was in the ICU as well, and if I could see her before I left.

"The looks on their faces should have told me everything, but one of the nurses, a really wonderful woman who had that kind of presence you associate with tough-love moms and fierce women fighting for equality, she uh…" I bite my lip a little and take a slow breath. "…she came and sat beside me. The other nurses backed out of the room and quietly closed the door. She took my hands, said some soothing words, but I just shook my head. It was like I couldn't hear correctly, like I had earplugs in and she was whispering.

"'I'm sorry,' I said, shaking my head. 'This is going to sound weird, but I can't hear you.'

"She looked at me for a long moment. Like that wasn't the first time someone had lost their senses and pushed the pain away, not even accepting it as actual words that made actual sound. She gripped my hands a little tighter and said, clearly and calmly…" I bite my lip again, looking to the ceiling.

Riaz looks at me, concern spreading into his eyes and rippling out to his eyebrows and the corners of his mouth. "You are preventing her from saying it even now."

I laugh without meaning to. It's not a fun laugh; it's cold and empty. I laugh because the jig is up, because he can see right through me, because he's right. I cannot bring myself to say the words. It's still too real, even after months, after grieving for her and for myself and for a life lived stopped in its tracks.

"No, I can't. Two words that changed everything. Sometimes I just blurt it out without thinking, other times, like now, I can't seem to let the words escape." I shrug and shake my head, for some reason disappointed in my fragility.

"She said, 'Sydney died,' didn't she?"

"Yes. Those two words," I confirm.

He sighs in return and we sit for a second in silence. He looks to the table, where the large file was sitting and flipped open the first few pages. "Her name was Marnie," he says quietly.

"That's right." It was strange to hear. I knew her name from before I heard the news. She had been really kind and we talked a lot while I was recuperating, but then I had just forgotten.

"Marnie." I roll the nurse's name around my mouth as if learning to speak again. "Yeah, Marnie." Somehow, solidifying her name in my mind gives me an anchor to the moment, to my memory, and allows me to step away from the grating, sharp pain of loss and instead see things from outside my experience.

"After Marnie told me," I continue, "I couldn't breathe. Everything started to spiral out of control. I remember her reaching out to steady me, her hands were still on mine, so she used one to grip my wrist hard, to pull me back towards the bed as the other hand went out, soccer mom style, to brace my shoulders and keep me from sliding to the floor.

"I don't remember hitting the floor, or falling onto the bed, or anything like that. Instead, I was suddenly, inexplicably back to a coffee date with my sister. I took a deep breath, a gasp even, when I first realized what was going on. Syd looked at me with concern, asking if everything was alright. It was just like the other lapse. It was real, not a memory. And there she was. She was reaching out just like Marnie had, with her hands gripping my hands as if they were the kite string and I was loose in the wind.

"All I could think was that I had suffered a horrible dream. Again, there were no casts, no wounds or bandages. Just me and Syd. Sitting at a table. I wanted it to be real. I wanted it so badly that I shook off all other feelings.

"'What were we talking about?' I asked her. She looked at me through pinched eyes, like that would help her see if there was a problem I was hiding, but after she seemed content that I was okay, she reminded me that we had been discussing the men in our lives.

"'You,' she said, 'were about to tell me that you have a crush on someone.' I looked at her incredulously.

"'Well, that's a lie,' I snapped back.

"That's when this homeless guy started to walk towards us. He said something about how nice it was to see us again, which was weird, of course, because we had never seen him before, but then he just sort of looks into the air beside me and starts talking to no one. 'I haven't seen you around before! Just try and stay calm.' It was strange. But something about it reminded me about that day, and I was suddenly aware what day it was for me and Sydney. It wasn't just any ordinary coffee, which we had all the time. 'Actually,...' I continued, trying to regain that moment, you know?"

Riaz nods, understanding how important that normal moment in our lives was to me.

"'Actually,' I said, 'I do think I have feelings for someone.'

"She got this look on her face that only a sister can get. It was part giddy, part inquisitive, and part protective. 'Uh huh,' she said, 'and who might that be?'

"I knew she would eventually get it out of me, and I knew that both in the real experience and in the lapse, and so I told her the same thing I had told her that day. 'Do you remember my friend Aaron from grad school?'"

Riaz's eyebrows go up. "Grad school?"

"Yeah, I did two years towards my Master's in Fine Art and then I realized I was never going to be able to repay the debt and it was going to be a worthless piece of paper for me."

"That can't be true," Riaz says in a mollifying way.

"I never got a chance to find out," I respond. "Anyway, she remembered I had talked about him, my friend Aaron. We had been best buds, we would go to the art supply store and gawk at the really nice materials and brushes and easels that we couldn't afford. We would eat burritos together at the same hole-in-the-wall place. So much so, in fact, that they would have his burrito ready by the time we got to the front of the lunch rush line."

A questioning look crosses Riaz's face. "But not yours?"

"Mine? Oh, my burrito. No, I didn't have a regular order. I changed it up every time, but Aaron was as predictable as a Swiss watch. Grande Pollo Asado Burrito Especial. To be fair, it was a damn good burrito."

"Noted," Riaz grins.

"Right," I continue. "So I told her about Aaron and how he had come to town and we'd had dinner the night before, or a couple of nights before, or whatever. He was moving to my neck of the woods and I offered him my second bedroom. Sydney was beside herself, half excited, half chastising me for bringing on a roommate that I had feelings for. It was one of those sister conversations where I would groan 'I know! I don't know what I was thinking!' and then she would get all conspiratorial and say 'Okay, but tell me everything, is he hot?'"

Riaz clears his throat a little and looks down at his note pad. "Right," he says.

I find his sudden awkward tension endearing. "Never had those conversations with your sister, huh?"

He shakes his head in return. "No, but perhaps I should the next time she tells me about a chap she likes. Which, come to think of it, she never has."

"You're missing out," I shake my head in mock disappointment.

"Well, was he?" Riaz asks, looking up from the pad to meet my eyes.

"Was he what?"

"Hot?"

My mouth falls open a little and I can feel the warmth of my embarrassment rising to my cheekbones. This causes Riaz to laugh out loud. "If you must know," I say, "yes, Aaron is very hot."

"As hot as the boys you would swoon over in high school?"

"I am regretting telling you all of that!" I hold my hands over my face for a second. With a deep breath, I sit up straighter and nod. "He was, and is, much hotter than those *boys*." I emphasize the last word to drive home the difference.

It's his turn to pink up a bit. "So, did you date him?"

"Off topic!" I quickly interject. "That isn't this part of the story."

"So it comes later then?" Riaz chides, a grin lighting up his features.

"That is not…" I throw my hands up a little and then continue. "In *this* part of the story, Syd was just finding out about Aaron moving to town. Then she told me she had a secret, too.

"'What is it?' I was leaning over the table to really get close to her and hear her dish the details.

"She smiled, but then her nose crinkled up and she bit her lip. It's this thing she does when she's nervous – like a poker tell. She knew I wasn't going to like her answer.

"'Oh no.' I shook my head at her. 'Who is it?' But I already knew. Because of the homeless guy, I knew what she was going to say.

"Then she told me, 'Do you remember that hot guy from the bar at Lucy's birthday party?'

"I did. Of course I did, and I didn't like where she was going with that, so I said, 'There were lots of hot guys there that night.'

"'Yeah,' she admitted, 'but do you remember *the* hot guy – the guy that bought me a Cosmo?'

"At this point I couldn't pretend I didn't remember. We had gone to our friend's birthday party at a bar and got a little tipsy and sung a few karaoke songs – "

Riaz's face lights up. "That must have been bloody brilliant! Please tell me what songs!"

With my eyes wide I purse my lips together in response. "Maybe someday," I barely squeak out. "That isn't the point either. The *point i*s that we were having a grand old time at the party and this guy walks up to us and props his elbow on our table, one of those high tables, you know?"

Riaz looks a little dejected that I won't tell him we were belting out Lady Gaga's greatest hits.

"Well, he puts an elbow down *between us*, facing her. Interrupts whatever I was saying and just slithers his way between us."

"Slithers," Riaz remarks.

"Yeah, can you believe that? This guy thinks he can just block me out of the conversation I'm having with *my sister* and try and sweet-talk her.

"Well, the short version is, he was an asshole. Arrogant, possessive, flashing his expensive watch and constantly name dropping and trying to demonstrate how awesome he was. Like he was some sort of catch." I shake my head. "But it worked. She was obviously way too drunk…"

"Obviously," Riaz agrees.

"Yes, and she falls for this asshole's lines and she only sees a handsome face, charming eyes, and God knows what else. The rest of us, and I do mean the rest of us, see him for the wormy little snake he really is. But it doesn't matter."

"That snake thing seems like it's going to be a recurring metaphor," Riaz offers.

"You would be right in so many ways. But anyway, she tells me, during this coffee date that I am reliving in the lapse, she tells me that she is dating that guy. Chrissss-topher." I practically hiss as I spit his name out.

"All sorts of things start running through my mind. I remember, suddenly and with perfect clarity, everything that happened from that moment to my reality in the ICU. I look up at her, wanting to slap some sense into her – " I pause, clarifying. "Not, like literally, just wake her up, you know? I am leaning towards her, about to tell her the crazy ridiculous future that I know, that I have lived, and the last thing I see is that same look of concern, and then I'm back in the hospital room with Marnie pumping air into my lungs, three other nurses buzzing around me, a doctor barking orders, and more of those sticky pads on my chest. At this point I'm pretty sure everyone in the hospital has seen my boobs." It's too late when I realize what I just said.

There is a palpable tension in the air between us as Riaz and I, our cheeks as red as apples, look anywhere but in the direction of the other. He runs his hand through his hair as though he can brush away the discomfort.

"And yet, despite all of that," I continue awkwardly, "I am more embarrassed at this precise moment than I was then."

Riaz puts his hand over his eyes shakes his head. "That makes two of us." He clears his throat, letting his hand fall as we both reluctantly make eye contact again.

"Sorry," I grimace.

"No worries. ICUs are weird like that. I understand that this particular lapse was exceptionally bad?" He smoothly transitions to a different topic, allowing both of us to ease our tense shoulders a bit.

"Yes," I continue gratefully. "I mean, you can see it all in the file, I guess. But my heart rate was really irregular, I was gasping like I was underwater, hence the oxygen mask thing, and basically everything was failing. Later, they told me I had suffered hypertension, hyperthermia, seizing, and arrhythmia. And what's more, I had to readdress the information about Syd's death." I pause. It's another of those times where I just blurt it out like that, *Syd's death*, and it was so nonchalant. It's almost harder to take than not being able to say the words at all.

Riaz looks me over, that same concern creeping into the creases above his nose.

"I was crushed," I manage. "Again."

Riaz is looking at the file again, writing more notes on his pad, which has five or six pages folded over the top and tucked back underneath. He's been writing more than I realized. He is scribbling notes, checking dates and statistics.

"Okay, so tell me if this sounds right." He leans back in his chair and rests the pad on his legs. "The first two lapses are triggered by extreme emotions and you go from a high stress situation in the 'now' to what was a high stress situation in your memory?"

I hadn't ever really thought about it. I shrug and gesture thoughtfully. "I think that is actually a pretty good assessment. I never realized that before."

Riaz leans forward with a little bit of excitement. "Okay then, let's test this theory out."

"Great!" I lace my fingers together and clasp my hands in excitement. "Wait." I stop and think for a second. "What theory, and how are we going to test it?"

- 12 -

TIMELINES

I have had MRIs before, once for a knee injury and once for my abdomen when an ER tech thought I might have appendicitis, but ever since the accident it seems like I have them once or twice a month. And now they're for my head. The doctors talk a lot about having set a baseline, but I keep thinking it can't be an actual baseline because they don't have the "before" image, only the "first" image. And the first image was taken after the accident.

But, apparently, the MRIs aren't what Riaz is interested in. Today will be something new – my first EEG. It feels more like a bad science fiction film than a routine medical procedure. There are electrodes stuck to my forehead and near my hairline and behind my ears, as well as a strange weave of electrodes in my hair. These are held in place with wires connected to some sort of central grid sitting on top of my head.

"I'm sorry for the stickies," Riaz offers as he continues to arrange the wires, gathering them into a sort of braid that he clips together. "I am used to an EEG electrode cap that just pops on and pops off. No stickies."

"Maybe you should have your lab send you an extra one," I mutter as my neck starts twitching at the strange sensation of the discs behind my ears.

"I just may, at that," he comes around to the front of me, leaning over a bit with his hands on his knees to be at my eye level in a partially reclined dentist's chair. "How's that?" he asks and I shrug.

"It is what it is. Let's get this party started!" I move my hands in a little circle in a mini dance and Riaz laughs.

"Let's." He heads to a chair next to a big computer display and some sort of control board and he starts typing and selecting different settings. He is clearly in his element, making concise decisions and adjustments on the complicated equipment.

"Okay." He turns back to me, swiveling in the chair. "For this first bit, we are just going to keep going with the stories of the lapses. Just so I can see what's going on in that brain of yours."

"Sure thing." I nod, a little clumsily with all the wires and sticky discs. "Ready when you are."

"Ready." Riaz picks up his notepad and flips the file open to a specific page.

"Okay, then." I continue with my story. "So. Lapse number three.

"After the second lapse, the doctors at the hospital thought I should be in a facility that could handle my issues, which I took to mean they didn't want to deal with me anymore."

"Probably true," Riaz smirks.

"Hey now!" I raise my eyebrows.

"Sorry," he says with a chuckle.

"Anyway," I emphasize slowly, "it was the day after I arrived here." I gesture to the room. "Well, not *here* here, in this little room. But, this building."

"I gathered that."

"Right, so I was in one of the nice rooms, with a window, because the others were all occupied, and I was looking out onto the freeway. All those cars moving in a flow, me stuck inside, the world forever changed. I sort of panicked, again."

"Understandable." This time there was no teasing in his voice.

"Yeah. Well, I was looking out and then I could see my reflection in the glass, and I just stared at myself and it's like I was in a loop looking at myself looking back at myself.

"The next thing I knew, I was looking in a mirror. But this mirror was in my apartment and I was in my favorite LBD – "

"LBD?" Riaz looks up, confused.

"Little black dress. Come on, man, you need to stop interrupting." He presses his lips together tightly, writes what I take to be a quick explanation of LBD in the margins of his legal pad and then gestures, poised for the continued story.

"Anyway, I was looking at myself, all dressed up, with my makeup done, my favorite necklace and earrings combo, and I was so confused. I just stood there, staring, expecting the reflection to turn back into the room with the freeway in the background.

"But instead, there was a knock on the bathroom door and I was suddenly aware that I had a date – well, I was meeting my sister and Christopher for dinner. But I had a plan." I press my fingers together in a conspiratorial way and drum them like a Bond villain.

"See, I was supposed to go alone, because Christopher liked to be in control of the situation, but I had already decided to bring Aaron with me."

"Aaron?" Riaz asks, adding nonchalantly, "The super-hot guy roommate person?"

"That's the one," I admit.

"So you did date him." Riaz grins in triumph.

I try to push right past my blushing and purse my lips together to stifle a flirty smile. "So it was him knocking, and he goes, right through the door, 'Come on already, Slowbie.'

"That's what he called me when I was, well, slow. So I looked back in the mirror, suddenly realizing this was another one of the episodes, and I decided to go along with it. The restaurant was a short walk from my apartment, our apartment, and I knew that the lapses didn't last very long, the memories I had experienced in the other two had given me ten or fifteen minutes of being in that place, so I was eager to get to the restaurant to see my sister.

"I had started to yearn for the lapses, you know? I wanted to see her. I was so lost without her that these little glimpses were the best thing I could have. I wanted to be there, I didn't want to be here.

"So I opened the bathroom door and I didn't even care whether or not Aaron thought I was cute, which I'm pretty sure I did in the real timeline."

"Interesting," Riaz muses. "That's the first time you have referred to your lapse memory as a different timeline."

"Well, you know what I mean. The real experience that I had versus the hallucination, or whatever. I did go through the motions like I normally do, said the words that popped into my brain, grabbed my clutch..." I pause when Riaz looks confused again.

"It's a type of small purse with no strap."

"Why wouldn't it have a strap? Wait, never mind, not important." He shakes his head.

"You really need to have a sit-down with your sister if you want to understand me better, because right now you are basically a clueless bachelor. The female mind is complicated enough without general male ignorance."

Riaz holds up a finger as if making a mental note. "So I should talk to Liyana?"

"For research," I suggest. "Also, because it's important to keep in touch with family, you know?"

"Right. I will make sure to call her tonight."

"Excellent. So remember, LBD and clutch. Start there and she should be able to guide you." I gesture at his legal pad and indicate he should be writing this all down.

He obliges me and writes it all down.

"At any rate, I grabbed Aaron and the clutch and ran out the door. He was taking forever, locking the door, putting on his jacket, all the while chastising me for taking forever in the bathroom only to be in such a hurry now.

"'I thought you didn't want to go to this dinner,' he said, and he quickened his stride to keep pace with me. It shouldn't have been an issue; I was in three-inch knock-off Jimmy Chu's..." My eyes dart to Riaz's face. "Put another note for Liyana," I suggest. "But somehow, he was nearly running as I was trying to get to the restaurant.

"It seemed like it took forever, but I was still there. Still in the midst of this memory and I knew where they were seated because I had been there before, had lived this all before, and I ran into the restaurant and raced past the hostess and straight to their table.

"Syd looked up and beamed at me, then she stood to match my enthusiasm at seeing her. That's something that always brightened my day, you know? She would be like an emotional accelerator. She would see me being happy or sad or angry and would match the emotion... or counteract it if necessary. It's hard to explain.

"But I couldn't believe I was still there. I was hugging her and didn't want to let go, but even given all the circumstances it became an awkwardly long hug. Especially because Aaron was standing behind me and, remember, he wasn't supposed to be there.

"That's where things got fun." I can't help but cackle.

"So, my plan in my real life was to have Aaron help me show Syd how much of a D.B. Christopher was."

"Another note for Liyana?" Riaz's eyebrows crane up in an adorable confusion.

"Not this time," I admit. "I don't know if other people say it or not, to be honest. It's just my shorthand for douchebag. Sorry."

Riaz shrugs and scratches another note in the margins.

"So the first fabulous annoyance that we created was the table situation. They had a small table pushed up against one of the walls in such a way that it could only fit three people. So, the wait staff and hostess had to work the table out and turn it sort of sideways to fit another chair. I sat between Christopher and Aaron so that Aaron could be a sort of counterpoint to Christopher for Syd. Chris was already pretty good at ignoring me and shouldering me out of the conversation, so I needed backup.

"Christopher would do little things, like interrupting, which I freaking can't stand." I shiver a little as the hairs on my neck prickle. Riaz, I realize, is looking at the monitors and information blinking on his screen.

"It was as if everything I had to say was meaningless, which was bad enough, but he did it to her as well. I couldn't understand why she didn't see it.

"So, anyway, I had primed Aaron for the situation with all of the things that Christopher did that drove me crazy, and the things that Syd should be upset about, and he starts double interrupting Christopher. When Sydney would be talking and Christopher would start to interject, Aaron would say something to reengage Sydney. He's quick-witted, too, so he was able to do it seamlessly.

"At first, Sydney was splitting her attention three ways, but then it was a tug of war between Chris and Aaron. I would try and do my part, asking Chris pointed questions so he would have to actively ignore me rather than answer, and sometimes I think he could smell it was a trap and he would kind of sneer and give me some annoying, dismissive answer, but all the while I couldn't help but smirk. Aaron was winning the attention war, and my little side skirmishes were helping. Christopher eventually did ignore me outright, but Sydney was captivated by Aaron, which I completely understand."

"A bit jealous, were you?" Riaz, writing on his notepad, doesn't look up, which I'm thankful for because I am flushed from head to toe.

"Maybe a little," I admit. "But my plan was working, so I wasn't thinking about Sydney falling for Aaron, I was thinking about Sydney not being with Chris.

"So then, in what I can only describe as a moment of desperation, Christopher grabs her chin, literally *grabs* her by the chin, and physically turns her face towards him. I couldn't believe it. Aaron couldn't either. We were both so taken aback, especially because Syd let him do it. I just felt this rush of fury and I could feel my heart pounding, and right as I was going to smack him square in the face, I got lightheaded, my sight grew blurry, and then everything sort of disappeared in a whoosh and I was back on a hospital bed, with nurses and machines and monitors all around me. And, for the first time, there was Dr. Strove."

"I see." Riaz scrunches his brow again. "You hadn't met him before then?"

"No, it was the first time. I think the era of having normal introductions to other people is behind me."

Riaz stifles a chuckle. "You do make a strong first impression."

I giggle self-consciously, remembering my first introduction to Riaz.

He looks over some of the data he's just collected, opens the massive file, and flips through Dr. Strove's notes. I think I can see a tinge of pink in his cheeks as well and I feel like a teenager, like when I swooned over the hot geometry teacher my sophomore year in high school.

"How long was the lapse?" he says more to himself than to me.

"They don't know." I snap out of my reverie and focus on the situation at hand.

He looks up at me. "Pardon?"

"They found me on the floor. I hadn't yet been hooked up to any machines or monitors or anything, so I was out at the very least longer than they marked."

Riaz flips through a couple of pages. "How long did it feel like it was?" he asks with a look of contemplation.

"Well, we managed to get to the restaurant, sit down, have appetizers and a drink, I think maybe the food had come. That would be, what, half an hour? Maybe forty-five minutes?"

Riaz nods to himself. "Interesting." He scribbles more notes on his pad and bites his lip in concentration, which I find unbearably adorable.

"Interesting in what way?" I nudge.

Riaz looks up like he forgot I was still here for a second. "Sorry, right." He flips back to a certain page in the file and turns the page to face me. "According to this, your lapse lasted at least thirty-two minutes from the moment they found you until you were able to be revived."

I look at the paperwork, but the information he is referencing is hidden in chicken scratch notes and stats listed on the medical form. "I'll take your word for it."

He spins the file around and looks at the information, regarding it as a layman would. "Right," he gives me a sheepish look. "Well, that's what it says. And these others..." he starts to say, flipping through the file towards the beginning. "The first was about ten minutes and the second about seven. Does that feel like it matches with the timeline in the memory?"

I think about the experiences with a new understanding. "Yeah, that's about right."

"That is very interesting."

- 13 -

DISPLAYS

Riaz closes the file and regards me for a second. I feel very much on display and start looking around the room awkwardly. Suddenly he seems jolted out of his contemplation and turns to the computer, clicking through several screens and scrolling through data that might as well be The Matrix as far as I can tell.

He leans back and crosses his arms. "Well, you are perfectly normal."

I cock my head and raise an eyebrow without meaning to. "I like to think of myself as above average."

He turns towards me and stares into my eyes for a tantalizing second. "That you are, without a doubt. But, of course, I am talking about your brain activity."

"Ah." I press my fingertips together as though I have a clue what normal brain activity is. "So, what does that mean?"

He thinks for a second and shrugs. "Whatever is happening during the lapses, it isn't leaving any trace in your brain. That is to say, there is no damage, no deterioration, no sign that anything has happened to your brain. But your body..." His eyes reflexively dart down my figure. We both seem to realize this at the same moment and he sits up straighter, eyes wide, and turns to the computer. I feel like giggling. The hot geometry teacher never checked me out. I bite my lips and raise my eyebrows as he talks at me over his shoulder.

"I mean your organs, vital functions, blood pressure…" He trails off as if he either doesn't know how to backpedal or recognizes its futility.

"Right. The hypertension, the damage to my heart, lungs, kidneys, all that stuff that Strove keeps saying."

"Right." He clears his throat. "Well, what this data is telling me is that if we want to understand what is going on, we need to observe you in an actual lapse, which is nearly impossible because they come with no warning or regularity. Merely having a conversation about an emotional subject doesn't seem to have created any anomalies. Which is good, but also not helpful."

"Okay, so…" I think I know where he's headed, but I don't love the idea.

"I think we need to figure out a way to track your lapses and see if we can find a pattern. And then we can figure out if we can plan for one. Try and get you monitored before, during, and after a lapse."

"Okay," I agree blankly. This was not what I was expecting. "But how are we going to manage that?"

"Well, you could keep a diary. If you lapse again – "

"When," I correct him.

"Right, when you lapse again, just write it down, everything you can remember, right after it happens." He looks at me. "Wait, let's get those off of you."

He walks over to me and starts to remove the braid of electrodes and disassemble the crown of cords. He is leaning over me and I'm right next to his chest. It's my turn to check him out. I feel somewhat uncomfortable, like I'm invading his privacy or treating him like a piece of meat, but I can't help it. He's in great shape, which I can see better now through the gap of his doctor's coat to his form-fitting t-shirt. His pecs are clearly outlined, though not in a body-builder way. Just in that athletic professional way that I apparently love. As his arms move around in front of me and he starts carefully peeling the sticky discs off of my forehead, I can see that the coat is stretched slightly around his bicep. My hand starts to reach up to stroke the length of his arm.

I realize what I'm doing and slam my hand back down in my lap.

"Are you okay?" He steps back to look me in the eyes.

"Yep. Just those darn sticky discy thingies," I giggle awkwardly.

I swear I can see the hint of a suppressed grin sneaking through his calm countenance. I wonder for an instant if he did this on purpose to even us out in terms of awkward ogling. He smells really good.

"Ouch!" I'm brought back to the moment, and the situation, as he pulls one of the stickies off of my neck.

"Sorry."

"Those little hairs are the worst!" I reach up to rub the tender spot where the electrodes ripped out some of my fine neck hairs. He carefully starts peeling the next sticky.

"I started reading that book you recommended," he mentions, easily distracting me from my slight discomfort.

"Which one? I don't remember suggesting anything."

"Oh, right, I mean after you said it was one of your favorites, I picked up a copy."

"I see," I say, with a tinge of sarcasm.

"What?" he asks. "You have good taste in books."

"Sure. And, I mean, you have to research my interests to make sure you understand my brain and all." I'm grinning like the Cheshire cat.

"Yes." He gestures in the air with his finger, like some sort of thoughtful movie professor. "It's a good way to figure out how you…" He looks sideways at me. "Yeah, no, it doesn't give me any insight into your brain. But it is a good book."

"So which one did you pick up?" The nature of the reclined chair left me turning my head to look up at him like some sort of film noir femme fatale.

"Ove," he says, looking back at me. "It's amazing." He stares at me, through me even, with a soft gaze. I wonder if he is only talking about the book.

"It is amazing." I don't mean to mirror him as much as I am, but I can't seem to control it. I lean in just a little and breathe more slowly. The spark between us is electric. The moment lasts for a few delicious seconds before he snaps out of it and brusquely clasps his hands together. "Right!" He pulls away from me like he's afraid he'll get burned. "We should be good, all the thingies are... off." His smile is forced, like someone trying to talk their way out of a speeding ticket.

I sigh slowly, straightening up in the chair. We're a hell of a pair – a broken brain case with no tangible future and her insanely hot doctor who is ethically bound not to pursue his patient.

For both our sakes, I try to change the subject. "He reminds me of Strove."

Riaz is busy tidying up the files and saving the information to a thumb drive. "What was that?"

"Ove. He reminds me of Dr. Strove. Hard-edged, cold exterior with a heart of gold."

Riaz nods with his back still turned to me. "Yes, they certainly do share some characteristics." He spins around with the file tucked up in his arms and the thumb drive clutched in his fist. "I'll walk you back to the ward. Ms. Griffin must miss you."

I try to stifle my sigh as I watch him walk to the door. He has a great ass, too. It takes me a second to realize he is holding the door open for me. *And he's a gentleman to boot.* I scamper out of the room before I embarrass myself again.

* * * *

Carrie gives me a questioning look as I turn to her after saying goodbye to Riaz. I can tell my expression must be giddy, but I can't help it.

"What the hell is going on between you two?" She crosses her arms and looks me up and down.

"Nothing!" I respond, too quickly, adding with a pout, "Unfortunately."

"Oh my God, you've fallen for him."

There's no use denying it. "One hundred and ten percent." I take a deep breath and hug myself just thinking about him.

Carrie has a tinge of pity in her voice. "You know it can never happen, though, right?"

It doesn't even dampen my mood. "I know," I respond. "But it's still nice to feel again. Nice to have conversations and share jokes and gaze into someone's eyes."

"My Lord." Carrie shakes her head. "You're going to get him in trouble. He could lose everything, you little siren. Plus, you're probably clinically insane, so you can't make those decisions. If you did end up together, he might be criminally liable. Leave the poor boy alone to do his work."

I can't help but scowl at her. "I am his work, Carrie."

"Ain't that a shame for the both of you."

She sits down and motions to the other side of the table. I walk over, expecting a lecture or a warning or some serious chastising. Instead, she starts dealing. I smile my biggest smile at her.

"Yeah, yeah," she mutters. "There's not much I can do to help either of you, so we might as well move on and play some cards."

We've been playing for ten minutes or so when one of the nurses comes in and hands me some blank sheets of paper and a pen.

"Dr. Choudhury asked me to give this to you," she offers. "He says you'll know what it's for."

As the nurse walks out, Carrie raises an eyebrow. "So, what is it for?"

"I think I'm supposed to keep a diary."

Carrie laughs. "Kid, just remember that those pieces of paper are going to be a part of your medical record."

That's a horrible thought. "Point taken," I say appreciatively.

- 14 -

ENGAGING

Despite everything that is happening, I've managed to find a rhythm and a bit of happiness in this situation. Yes, it turns out that I have fallen for my doctor, which is vastly inappropriate, but he is a good conversationalist and he feels like a partner in this adventure. Plus, I have Carrie, I have Office Building TV, and I have paper and a pen now, which has proven to be very engaging.

Carrie is bored, absentmindedly flicking through the books on the sad little bookshelf, as we wait for the dinner trays to be brought up to the game room from wherever the kitchen is in this place. "Seriously, you would think they could spring for a few new books every year, at least."

She abandons the shelf, with its few romance novels, the Bible, *Huckleberry Finn*, and *Stranger in a Strange Land*.

"I miss books," I say distractedly as I sketch the roundness of a shoulder on the figure I'm drawing.

"I thought that was supposed to be for writing." She gestures to the paper.

"And it is. Or, rather, the other pieces of paper are. They are so stingy with supplies."

Carrie looks over my shoulder down at the piece of paper. "That's not half bad," she says admiringly.

"Thanks. I almost got my MFA, you know."

I can tell Carrie is looking me over from the way her posture seems to shift.

"What?" I drop my pencil and turn to face her.

"I feel there is a whole other issue we need to address about your 'almost' life, for when you get out of here."

"If."

"When," she corrects, moving to sit at another chair around my table. "Until then, you should definitely keep drawing. You can make a comic of our lives watching the lives of others."

"I'll run out of paper before then," I sigh.

"It does make you wonder what the heck they think we're going to do all day. Reread the same eight books, play cards with incomplete decks, watch snow on the broken TV with no cable. Hell, even the *Sorry!* game is missing pieces. You'd think we could at least have some paper to make our own damn entertainment."

"Getting tired of your extended stay in sterile hell?" I pick up my pencil again and start sketching the outlines of her face, now in a scowl.

She glowers. "A little. How are we supposed to stay engaged? Entertained? Alive?"

I flutter my eyelashes. "I find my treatment very engaging at the moment."

"Fine, you can flirt all you want, but what am I supposed to do?"

"Do you even need to be here? I still don't know why you are. I mean, I am grateful, don't get me wrong," I quickly interject, "but how does Strove justify your medical status?"

She looks crestfallen, but only for a split second. It passes so quickly I think I must have imagined it. "Well, he has his ways." She coughs a bit, lightly.

"Ha ha," I mock in a droll tone, thinking she's faking it. She coughs again, but this time it's deep and coarse. "Carrie?" I drop my pencil onto the table and focus on her. "What's the matter?"

"It's nothing." She tries to reassure me, but as she takes a breath the cough returns violently.

I rush to her side and grab her tightly around the shoulders as she shakes, nearly losing her balance. She looks up at me, shock and fear spreading over her face.

"What is it? What's going on?" I can hear the panic in my own head as I try to calm my voice so as not to alarm her more.

"Your monitor!" She grabs my wrist hard.

I didn't even hear it beeping. To me it's like a newscast in another room, where you can only pick up a few fleeting moments of conversation. I shake my head and ignore the beeping. She starts to cough again and I pull my wrist away from her, focusing my attention back on her, even as my vision begins to blur at the edges.

She is trying to speak to me past the coughing spell, but I can't understand her words. I may not have been able to, anyway, as I am breaking with the present reality despite my best efforts.

When the unexpected hands of the nurses take hold of me, I resist. I'm trying to swat at them. I need to tell them that it isn't me who needs help, it's Carrie. But she's reaching out to me as well. She seems to be in charge, barking orders at a nurse near the door; the nurse rushes out, holding her ID badge to her chest so it doesn't bounce as she runs.

I try to stay. I try not to drift away. I try to anchor my entire conscious focus on Carrie.

But it doesn't work.

* * * *

When the haziness clears, I am now the one coughing violently. I can feel there is something in my throat, in my windpipe trying to drive its way into my lungs. My eyes are squeezed tightly shut as I try to force the foreign substance out.

A solid smack on the back pulls me into the moment, and I open my eyes to find myself staring at Aaron. He rubs my back and says something, but I can only see his lips move. I can't hear him. I can't focus. I'm thinking about Carrie, about her cough, hoping that this memory … no, this lapse … has arisen to remind me that coughing violently doesn't always mean something is wrong. Just a little liquid down the wrong pipe.

I take a deep breath, and look back to Aaron. "What was that?"

He grimaces and lightly pats my back again. Now I can hear him. "You had us worried."

Us.

Transitioning from the real to the lapse is mired in haze and confusion and split focus, and the fog seems to be getting worse, the transition rougher each time it happens. But now more fully in this lapse, I take the opportunity to look around.

Aaron is in his nice blazer that he wears when we go out. No, wore when we went out. That night.

My eyes meet Sydney's, then roll around to an annoyed-looking Christopher. "Maybe drink more slowly," he mocks, taking a slow and exaggerated sip of his wine.

"Thanks for the advice." I can't contain the venom in my words.

"Whoa, let's not get nasty. Can't you two get along?" Sydney tries to lighten the tension, making it seem like we were both joking. In an effort to please her, which we are both eager to do, we each force a smile.

Aaron shoots Christopher an irritated glance but turns his attention back to Sydney. With Syd momentarily distracted, Christopher and I stare daggers at each other, returning to faux contentment before she can look back at us. I hate this man so much.

Aaron and Sydney are discussing some story that just came out about potential bacteria and amoebas found under the ice on Europa, and I don't want to interrupt them. But I need to, because I know that Christopher is about to.

"Did you ever see that movie?" Aaron and Syd both look at me in mild shock. I always try my best not to interrupt people. I hate it as much as Sydney does. "Sorry to interrupt, but *Europa*. That movie?"

Syd breaks her eye contact with Aaron, looking back and forth between him and me. "I think maybe. Why?"

"No, I mean, it's just that in the movie that's the question they are exploring, you know? Whether or not there is life under the ice on Europa. It's awesome."

Syd gives me a knowing glance and as Aaron and Christopher both look at me, she mouths the word "sorry" and I am suddenly very confused. Then she pulls her hand off of the table, where she had been resting it to lean in to speak with Aaron and I get it.

"No, that's not what I meant." I try to correct her thinking, but I am getting foggy already. It's clear she thinks I'm jealous of her interaction with Aaron. And I am, or I was, but I have more important things to worry about. "No, it's just that..." I look back and forth between them, trying to remember what I was going to say.

"It doesn't matter," Christopher rudely breaks into the silence, taking Syd's hand in his. "We have an announcement."

"Now?" Syd whispers, looking sheepish.

Christopher doesn't even acknowledge her discomfort.

"No." I shake my head. *Am I supposed to stop this?*

"Yes," Christopher continues, annoyed. "We're engaged."

He doesn't say it with the eager, love-filled excitement of the newly engaged. Rather, he says it as a kind of declaration, like he is hammering a fence down around her. And he isn't looking at me when he says it, he is staring Aaron down.

I remember it all.

This was the night that I lost control of everything. This was the night that Sydney succumbed to Christopher's manipulation, the night my battle with him was lost, and the night I realized that Aaron – my best friend, roommate, and crush – was in love with someone else.

- 15 -

DETERIORATION

My head is reeling, but I can't do anything about it. I didn't do enough back then, when I had the chance. At moments like this, I didn't try to make her see. I need to make her see. Maybe…

"No!" I slam my fists down on the table, forcefully shaking the stemware.

Syd looks shocked and a little angry. "Taylor, honestly," she starts.

Aaron's eyes dart between me and Syd, and Christopher looks so furious I think he could snap my neck.

"No," I continue, cutting her off. "You have to be joking. This guy?"

"Taylor!" Sydney shouts, her expression sours into fury.

"Maybe we should go get some air," Aaron says, placing his napkin on the table.

"No!" I scream again, but I can feel my blood pressure, can feel the rush of emotion, the strings of reality pulling on me. "I didn't say anything that night and it's all my fault! You know I'm right!"

Syd looks to Aaron with slight accusation and his eyes get bigger as he tries to help me up, flushing with embarrassment and trying to avoid the heat of Christopher's gaze.

I can feel my chest get tight, Aaron trying to pull me to my feet.

"You have to help me!" I plead with him.

The last thing I see is a genuine look of concern on Aaron's face as he takes both my hands in his. A pain in my chest, like a shock of lightning coursing through my veins, catches me off guard and I squeeze my eyes shut.

* * * *

I can't breathe, like my lungs have collapsed. It's as if they can't open and let oxygen in. My head throbs and I have pains in my back, my sides, every joint and muscle feels on fire.

Another shock forces me to open my eyes and I look around to see several nurses working feverishly. I'm on the floor of the game room, my heart is beating erratically; they've brought in the defibrillator, there's an oxygen mask over my nose and mouth, but it still feels like I can't get air into my lungs, and tears are streaming down my cheeks.

For a moment, everything is so bright I can't focus on the individual figures racing about me, but soon my vision returns and I search the room frantically for Sydney, which I immediately realize is insane. Then I am searching for Carrie.

A nurse is helping her with her own oxygen mask. I feel as though our expressions are mirrored, each of us searching out the other, assessing each other's well-being in spite of our own difficulties.

She nods to me and I am overcome with wrenching, gasping sobs. My lungs burn as they finally fill with air. The emotional toll of these lapses is greater every time. The further away I get from Syd, the more the lapses provide the grace of seeing her again and the torment of reliving my greatest loss. Watching Carrie in trouble on top of that is too much.

The nurses carefully remove the defibrillator pads and the burns under them sting as they suddenly meet the chill air of the room. One of the nurses pulls the sides of my hoodie together over my bare torso and places her hand reassuringly on my chest, then pulls the zippers together. Other nurses are gathering my vital signs and focusing on keeping me alive.

Dr. Strove is there, splitting his focus between me, Carrie, and ordering the nurses around. A gurney is rolled into the room and with the nurses' help I am situated onto the stiff mattress. As they roll me out of the room, I crane my neck to get one last glimpse of Carrie and she leans into view to wink at me before quickly disappearing behind the nurses. I'm mentally, emotionally, and physically exhausted. The bright fluorescent lights of the hallway drift past, and I let the fear and grief and anger sweep over me as I lose consciousness beneath the monotony of drop ceiling tiles.

* * * *

When I come to, it is dark in my room, but the slightly purple light coming from the windows on the other side of the hall tells me it's either dusk or dawn, not actually night. There isn't much activity at the nurses' station, so I guess it's early morning, and I take a slow, deep breath to test out my aching lungs.

"You're awake." A groggy voice in the corner draws my attention back into my room.

"Sort of," I rasp, my lungs and throat still feeling ravaged by the prior day's episode.

Riaz stands up from a too-small hospital chair and places his hands in the small of his back to aid in a long stretch.

"How long have you been here?" It's hard to speak, and I feel the need to roll my tongue around my teeth in a vain attempt to wet them.

"A while," he says vaguely, stepping closer to my bed. "I missed all the fun."

It's too soon for me to joke about it, so I just look away from him and try another slow, wavering breath. I can feel the corners of my eyes moisten.

"Sorry," he quickly apologizes, taking my hand in his. "I shouldn't have said that."

"I think I'm getting worse," I whisper.

Riaz doesn't respond, he just squeezes my hand a little tighter.

It's enough of a response to tell me he agrees.

- 16 -

DEPENDENCE

He stands there for a while, simply holding my hand. We are comfortable just being for a moment. Just letting the air pass between us as we each contemplate my condition in our own way.

"Here." Riaz pulls something out of a folder and starts to hand it to me. "I found these on the table. I thought you might like them back."

It's the drawings I was sketching right before the last lapse. The top image is the half-completed sketch of Carrie's scowl. I let my fingers trace the thin graphite lines.

"They're really good. Like, really really good. Brilliant, in fact. I think you could make a great career with an MFA, if you ever decide to go back." His shoulders sink a little. "Just saying, you are really talented."

"I was going to be a graphic designer."

After a while, but without looking in his direction, I manage to ask, "Is Carrie alright?"

"I don't know," Riaz admits. "I am here to observe you and what goes on in your fascinating brain. Ms. Griffin is not my patient."

I turn to look him in the eyes, unable to put on any expression to mask my fear and grief. He takes my hand again. "I will find out and let you know."

I nod in reply and take another slow breath, closing my eyes to try and will my body to heal.

"Right now, though," he says, letting go of my hand to pull the chair closer to my bedside, "I need to know what happened."

I gesture meekly with my hand. "May I have some water first?"

"Of course." Riaz stands and briskly walks out of the room, returning shortly with a thin plastic cup with a bending straw.

"Wow, the fancy straws." I try a smile. It probably doesn't even look like one, though.

The tension in Riaz's face softens. "Only the best for my patients."

I take a sip, slowly, very conscious of the coughing fit I had in the lapse, and of the one that Carrie had in the game room. I don't want to cough for a while.

"It's going to..." – I have to wait for the pain in my throat to subside – "...be a minute."

He nods.

"How is Liyana?" I venture, trying to get him to do some of the talking while my throat heals.

He lights up enthusiastically. "She is doing well. Has a chap in her life, which I asked and she actually told me."

I eagerly wait for more information, but he is not forthcoming. "And?"

"Well, from what I can tell he sounds like a good one. I suppose I can't really know without meeting him, but she seems smitten. She asks about you."

My eyebrows go up. "Is that legal?"

"I don't share your medical history with her, if that's what you mean. I just mentioned that I'd made a friend out here and she started whittling all the information out of me."

"Little sisters do that." My throat is starting to feel a little better. "So what does she say?"

"About you?" Riaz looks a little nervous.

"Yes." I give him my most serious face until I break into a wide grin.

"She thinks you and I would have been the best of mates as teenagers. And she is convinced you and she would get along swimmingly as well."

"I think that's probably true."

He tells me some more about Liyana's new boyfriend, and about her new job, as that is how she met the new boyfriend. He talks until I'm calm and speaking more easily.

"Are you good?" he asks, even though I'm sure he already knows.

After a few slow sips of water I look up at him. "What would you like to know?"

He sets the cup down on a mobile table and picks up my growing file, which has been sitting on the floor by the wall where it seems he must have slept in the hospital chair. He flips open his notepad to an empty sheet and looks up. "What do you remember?"

What do I remember? I remember everything, I want to tell him. I remember all the frustration and anger and fear. I shake my head. "I went back to the night Christopher told us they were engaged."

Riaz writes something down. "Us?" he asks for clarification.

"Aaron and I. We had dinner with them again, despite Christopher's best efforts to get Syd all to himself." I can't help but laugh a little. "You should have seen his face when we got there."

"Again? So you didn't go back to the same lapse as before? The table against the wall that had to be moved?"

Things are still groggy. His questions confuse me, but then I remember the different dinners and different nights. "No, a different night. Good memory, though," I grin. "This was maybe a month later? Christopher had avoided dinners with us for a while, but I think he knew he couldn't put us off forever. Eventually, if he didn't give in, Syd would just force us all to get together, which would make him look bad. Anyway, it was the night he told us they were engaged." I shake my head. "This lapse was different."

"Different how?" Riaz asks, his pen poised above the pad but his attention fully on me.

"Different because I didn't follow the script."

"How do you mean?"

I shake my head, the whole of it is so fuzzy. "That night, in reality, with Aaron and Syd and Dumbass, I was mortified, I was angry, but I was polite. I didn't say anything. I just drank my wine and clenched my fist under the table. But in the lapse, I was not polite."

Riaz can't help but lean in. "You told Dumbass where he could shove it?"

It is meant to be a joke, I realize, but something different had happened and it's important, I just can't quite put my finger on why. "Yes," I finally admit. "I sort of did."

Riaz looks at me skeptically. "And this bothers you, somehow?"

"It bothers me because they have always been memories, you know? Like, I have relived the moments, but followed the same path, the same words, the same steps."

"The same script," Riaz repeats.

"Yes."

"But have you really?"

This catches me off guard. "Yes, of course."

"But what about the previous dinner? You said that you ran to the restaurant to be with Sydney, that Aaron kept asking why you were in such a hurry – "

"Right, but I did hurry that night…" I put my hand to my head. "I think I did."

"I got the impression you behaved contrary to your original reality. Your first 'timeline' as you put it."

My head starts spinning. I am not sure. I remember both versions of that recollection, but running feels like the memory and an ordinary cheerful walk with Aaron seems more like the dream. I think I ran into the restaurant, but now a calm, mischievous plan, executed with poise, seems like the dream. My head is aching.

"I can't quite remember."

Riaz drops the file and legal pad on the floor by the chair and stands next to me, looking into my eyes the way a doctor does. He pats his pockets and curses under his breath, clearly missing some device he wishes he had.

"I think it would be best if you rested a little more," he says, peering into my eyes without the aid of whatever tool he was looking for. "We can pick this up tomorrow."

"Right," I say, trying to blink away my confusion by squeezing my eyes shut tightly over and over and shaking my head.

He rests his hand on mine gently. "We'll figure this out. I promise. Oh, I almost forgot." He reaches into one of his deep pockets and pulls out a small leather-bound journal. "I thought this might be easier to keep track of than a bunch of loose papers. I was out getting it earlier when… everything happened. I think I need to head to the hotel for a bit and clean up, but I would like you to jot down what you remember and we can get back to this tomorrow or the next day. Take your time and rest. I have plenty of other things I can do to try and figure out your incredibly complex brain." He hands me the journal. "I'll check in on you soon."

I carefully reach out, taking the journal as if it is the most precious thing anyone has ever given me. I can't think of anything to say as he gathers his things and heads for the door.

"Thank you," I finally manage as he turns in the doorway.

"You're welcome." He pats his hand on the doorframe a few times as if he wants to say something else, but then shakes his head to himself, giving a small wave as he heads down the hall.

* * * *

I don't need a doctor to tell me I'm getting worse. The duration, severity, and frequency of the episodes are all increasing, and my body can feel it.

Everything aches slightly, but my lungs, heart, and kidneys are the worst. I can feel them; they're like large splinters jammed into my body and they feel foreign and out of place. I never knew it could be so disconcerting to feel every pumping beat of your heart or know the exact location of your kidneys because of the constant ache.

I don't even want to get out of bed yet, and the medical staff doesn't seem to have any plans for me along those lines. I am bedridden, at least for the time being. At least this time I'm not strapped in, just unable to move under my own power.

The nurses come in more regularly, and they have softened towards me, though I don't know why. That almost scares me more than anything, because they clearly know something I do not.

Riaz and Dr. Strove also come in more regularly, though both of them seem more concerned with my medical situation than with my mental one. Riaz, I think, didn't really understand what it was like when I lapsed. There were charts and statistics and data, but on paper is different than in the flesh. Even without being here for the actual lapse, he clearly sees that I am altered as a result. He had ordered another MRI and more x-rays and he often discusses the results with Dr. Strove at the nurses' station or the lightbox on the hallway wall. They both can't hide their concern anymore and I feel like one of them is always nearby, even if I can't see or hear them. Apparently, the strain of the last lapse re-cracked one of my ribs, either from my thrashing or the nurses' actions. One of the reasons it hurts to breathe, I imagine.

* * * *

It's no surprise when Riaz walks in, but it is unusual when he pulls the chair from the corner of the room to the side of the bed and sits down.

"To what do I owe the pleasure?" I manage a weak gesture to the chair.

Riaz smiles broadly in return. "I have a theory, but I would like some more information."

105

"Exciting stuff." I take a slow, deep breath, trying not to wince when my ribs expand.

"Still in pain? I can prescribe something that might help. Or I can order a sleep aid, if you like."

I shake my head. "Nah. I'd rather not mess with the cocktail of my brain chemistry any more than absolutely necessary."

He sighs. "Okay, then."

He looks tired. His eyes flick over the bruises on my arms from where the nurses pulled me away from Carrie; he takes in the slight burn from the defibrillator peeking out from the V-neck collar of my gown.

"Don't worry," I try to assure him. "I bruise easy."

"You shouldn't be bruised at all." He shakes his head. "We need to figure this out sooner rather than later."

"Agreed. So what information can I give you today?"

"Well, if you're up to it, I would like to keep going with the discussion of the lapses."

"Do you really think it will help?"

He seems earnest when he nods. "Yes, of course. I think I might be able to come up with a solution, but I need to have more context for what causes the bloody things. Why do they happen when they do? Why do you 'return' to certain memories and not others? Are they at all predictable, or are they completely random?" His normally calm demeanor is gone; he's clearly agitated, the muscles in his neck and jaw tense.

I want to do anything I can to help him, whether or not it will make a difference in my limited future. "Well, I've not got any other plans today." I try to sit up and he stands to help me adjust a pillow behind my back. "Thanks." I am grateful, but also feeling sheepish to be so vulnerable. I preferred it when I was a strong, independent woman who thought she didn't need anyone. But that was back when I had a job, an apartment, a roommate, and a sister. And an unbroken brain.

"Not at all." Riaz sits back down, his tension abating slightly. "So, where were we?" He flips open his legal pad, which looks to be almost halfway full of notes, and reads the last page, murmuring to himself, before looking up at me. "I think we are up to lapse number four."

I shake my head in agreement. "You would think I would lose track, but I still remember each of them." I get the story straight in my head and take a slow, deep breath. "Okay, so lapse number four was the second one I had here, and they didn't know what to do with me yet, so I was continually strapped into a bunch of machines. They were monitoring all sorts of things that proved irrelevant and massively invasive, but let's just skip right over that.

"This fourth lapse didn't have as much of a trigger as the others. I was just suddenly overwhelmed with it all. There was tapioca pudding on the tray, which I hate, and I hate eating in bed, and I felt like everything was getting worse – little did I know it could be so much worse – but something about the tapioca set me off. I know that sounds nuts." I shake my head.

"Not at all. That slop is pure rubbish."

I giggle, wince in response to the sharp pain in my chest, and hold my breath for a second. "Don't make me laugh," I plead jokingly, the corners of my mouth still twitching upwards.

"My apologies!" Riaz looks mortified.

"Ow ow ow! Your face!"

He sits back, relaxing a little, and raises an eyebrow. "My face is that hilarious?"

"Only when you look gobsmacked."

"Well, I will try to be less concerned with your welfare and less responsive to your story. Not to mention less hilarious."

Or irresistibly handsome, I think to myself, keeping my eyes closed while I breathe through the pain and picture the way his lab coat stretched over his bicep when he removed the EEG stickies. I let out a long sigh.

"Right," I continue. "Well, there I was, staring at that complete rubbish…" I crinkle up my nose for effect. He holds back a chuckle. "… and I felt sort of lost. I felt like I was fainting, like I had donated too much blood and tried standing up, you know? It was like a whoosh of bright light and then I was stumbling up a driveway. I had to stop because I had gone from hospitalized and hooked up to a ton of machines to walking, unencumbered, in the sun on a beautiful day. It was massively disorienting.

"I had to take stock of my surroundings. I was carrying a canvas workbag with a few trowels, little forked weeder thingies, and a half-open bag of planting soil. And then it hit me. I actually thought to myself, *Are you freaking kidding me? I have to relive this bullshit?*

"Because I knew exactly what day it was. And I didn't need a lapse to remember it, because I had been thinking about it every day.

"This was the day that I went to drop off some of Syd's gardening stuff back at her house. I didn't expect anyone to be there, I was just going to drop it off in her shed and text her, but when I got to the back yard, I realized there was movement in the house.

"My first thought was that a burglar had gotten in, because I used to watch way too much crime TV, so I snuck a little closer to get a better look."

"You must be joking," Riaz exclaims. "If it had been a burglar, which I'm fairly certain it wasn't, you could have been killed! What on earth were you going to do?"

"I hadn't thought that far forward! Besides, that was in my past and we are talking about a *lapse*, remember?"

Riaz quickly shakes his head. "Right, sorry. I was just so baffled by your actions. And now, after I said your brain was perfectly normal, I have to learn about this."

I scowl. "Yeah, yeah. It wasn't exactly my smartest moment, but I didn't go barging in, I just went to investigate."

"Still fairly dangerous, but go on." Riaz poises his pen over his notepad.

"Fine," I continue. "Anyway, I look into the house and to my complete horror, it was Christopher, walking around the kitchen in a towel. I almost retched. That is not something I ever wanted to see, let alone relive. But I had snuck past some bushes, so I couldn't just run away, I had to extract myself."

Riaz starts to shake his head, but I don't give him the opportunity to say anything.

"And that is when I saw her."

"Sydney?" Riaz interjects.

"Nope."

Riaz's eyes widen. "You don't mean – "

"Oh, I do mean. There, coming down the stairs, wearing nothing but one of his button-down shirts, is some bimbo. The asshole is cheating on my sister, not even a year into their marriage."

"You have to be bloody kidding me." Riaz's disgust starts to mirror my own.

"Oh, I'm dead serious. But, see, I am not a subtle person by nature – "

Riaz interrupts with a laugh. "Oh my God, what did you do?"

"Well, I was still in the bushes, so I banged on the glass, screaming at him and calling him every name in the book. I ripped through the bushes, throwing some of the branches back towards the house as I marched around to the back door, then I was pounding on the glass.

"I was so in the moment that when I started to get blurry-eyed, I assumed it was rage induced, but then it hit me that I was in the middle of a lapse and I wanted to change it, call Syd, text her, anything, but it's too late and I am slipping back to the hospital bed.

"As I'm sure my file says, I had really high blood pressure and I was breathing hard and my body was acting like I had just gone for a three-mile sprint. Which, I think, is exactly how I felt on that actual day, when I found out he was cheating. When I came to, I was so mad that my blood pressure didn't return to normal for an hour.

"So, to your theory, that was definitely an emotional and stressful memory, though I can't tell you why the tapioca would have set me off that much."

"Yeah, it's terrible tapioca, but not Christopher terrible."

"Yes! Thank you! That's what I think, too."

Riaz sits back. I didn't realize until now that he had been sitting on the edge of his seat. It doesn't even seem like he took any notes, even though his pen is still in his hand. He was just listening to my story, intently.

"Right," he says. I relax a bit myself. I always get tense when I think about that day, not to mention talk about it. My tension has caused my recent injuries to flare up, so I actively try to release my muscles. "Well, all I can tell you is that the whole thing took less than ten minutes, but affected me for days."

Riaz turns to the folder and flips to a sticky note protruding from the rest of the papers. "It was…" – he scans the page with his fingers, tapping on the paper when he finds what he was looking for – "eight and a half minutes."

"That's so weird that the times align," I muse.

"Very strange, but also very interesting. I'm hoping that in figuring you out, we might actually be able to hypothesize about how the unconscious mind perceives time differently than the hallucinating mind. You can live a lifetime in a split second in a dream, but hallucinations in the conscious mind, whether visual or auditory, are often time dependent. I have assumed that hallucinations in the *unconscious* mind should behave like dreams, but somehow you are maintaining a connection to the conscious while deeply entrenched in memory with hallucinated hyper reality."

"Holy crap!" It's the first time Riaz has tried to articulate his theory to me, and it's a lot to take in.

"I mean, it's still just a theory," Riaz assures me, putting his hands out in a vain attempt to soothe me.

"Okay." I'm shaking a little and I can hear a few beeps from the machines behind me. "So what does that mean?"

Riaz has stood and his attention is going back and forth between the machines and me. "Sorry, I didn't mean to throw all of that at you at once, I was just very intrigued by the whole thing and lapse number four falls into the same pattern." He is frantically writing something down on the back of a sheet of paper in the large folder. Two nurses come rushing in, but he waves them off, saying, "We're good. We're doing fine."

The nurses look to me and I shrug and they turn and walk out. Nurse Now-Blue-Nails shoots a distrusting glare at Riaz's back as she leaves. It takes me by surprise, as it seems she is looking out for me. It's an unexpected connection, but I find that it relaxes me and the beeps subside and finally quit.

Riaz takes a deep breath and blows out a sigh. "Sorry."

"It's fine." I take a slow breath myself. "But, seriously, what does that mean?"

"I think it means we need to figure out how your memory is triggering the lapses. While there are factors on this side of the equation, like waking in the hospital after the accident or finding out about your sister's death, that would certainly affect the balance of your brain chemistry, the tapioca and the reflection in the window don't seem like strong enough triggers. I think it is your memory that is driving this train."

My memory. If that's the case, I have plenty of traumatic life experiences to relive in hyper-realistic unconscious hallucinations until one of them finally kills me.

- 17 -

DUES

When Riaz returns the next morning, I am more alert and eager to get out of bed. If for no other reason than to find Carrie. She hasn't come to visit me. The nurses and Dr. Strove have been reluctant to discuss her with me since this most recent lapse, and they keep telling me that I need to focus on myself now.

Riaz, though, promised to find something out for me. And I intend to hold him to that promise.

He is barely through the door when I prop myself up on my elbows and bombard him. "Is Carrie okay? What is going on with her?"

Riaz first looks surprised, then sighs in resignation. He pulls the chair over and sits reluctantly. With that doctor expression that steels you for the worst news, he replies simply, "She's taken ill."

Taken ill. Like she somehow pulled something off the shelf while shopping. Like it was a choice she made.

"What do you mean? Ill with what?" I study his face for cracks in the façade, but he isn't giving anything away.

"I mean she is being cared for in her room, like you are being cared for in yours. I can't tell you more than that right now."

"Why?!" I am angrier than he expects.

He places a hand gently on my arm. "I am legally and ethically prevented from discussing her condition with you. But I promise that when one of you is well enough to leave her room, we will coordinate a visit. Okay?"

Now I feel like I'm a toddler asking for a play date.

"Fine, I'm ready, let's go." I try to pull back the thin blanket and sheet, but he stops me.

"Hold on." He sighs. "You are still attached to a lot of equipment and, as your doctor, I am not comfortable with you moving just yet."

"Just yet?" I scowl towards him.

"Just yet," he repeats, a look of stubbornness settling into his features.

I lower myself back onto the bed slowly.

"Would you like to sit up?"

I nod and he pushes the little button that makes the back third of the bed tilt up so that I can be in a sitting position.

"So what am I supposed to do in the meantime?"

Riaz settles back into his chair and picks up the folder and legal pad that he had placed on the floor. "We still have work to do. And, I think you would agree, we are making progress. Now, I want to focus on the events as well as the dates and times of those events to see if we can establish some sort of pattern."

"Right." I am less than eager today, though he still has a look of anxious curiosity.

"So," I continue, "you want to hear about the next lapse?"

"I do," he says. "I am curious about the medical implications of this complex history that you are reliving in your lapses."

"Medical implications?" I question, noting that he looks a little embarrassed.

"Yes, well, the more information, the better, right?"

"You just want to know what happened in the story, don't you?!"

He smiles sheepishly. "Not only..." he shrugs. "But yes. Please continue."

I can't help but relax a little. If I can't check in on Carrie, maybe I can at least pass the time with Riaz.

"Okay, so the next lapse happened a few days later."

"Yes, I see it was not even 72 full hours."

"Right," I agree. "Which is interesting because the event I lapsed to was only a few days after I caught Christopher cheating."

"Wait." Riaz stops me. "Are you saying that the timeline between lapses is matching the historical timeline?"

I think about it for a second. "That would be insane. But, no, I don't think it's precisely the same, just a coincidence."

"Interesting. Continue." Riaz scribbles something down, flips through the file and scribbles something else.

"Okay, so I was having another generally depressed day. I don't remember a trigger of any sort, but I felt the lapse coming. At this point I was starting to become familiar with the warning signs. I knew I couldn't control it, so I went with it. I just let myself drift off.

"When I fully entered the lapse, I was with Syd at that little café we like to go to. The transition was much smoother – no panic, no confusion, just like opening your eyes after lying in the sun for a while. Everything is a little out of focus, the colors are a little different, but after a second, everything goes back to normal.

"It was such a smooth transition that I just took a deep breath and sighed, listening to Sydney mid-story about some Zoom meeting she had been on with a colleague.

"She was saying, 'He was muted but he must have thought the camera was off too, and he starts picking his nose! Can you even believe that? Oh, it was mortifying.'

"I burst out laughing. 'Did you tell the poor guy?'

"'No!' She seemed affronted. 'What was I supposed to say? "Hey, Dave, we can all see your finger up your nose, mining for gold"?'

"I made a gagging noise, 'Ew, gross!' I couldn't help but giggle. 'Did he eat it?'

"This time Syd gagged. 'You're so disgusting!'

"I was laughing a full belly at this point. You know, the type that just shakes you and somehow relieves all the tension you're carrying. 'I'm just saying! Kristoff says all guys do it.'

"We always loved the Disney movie *Frozen* so the reference wasn't lost on her," I say to Riaz as an aside.

"She shrugged with faux resignation and said, 'Well, Kristoff does say so.'

"And then, at the same time, we both start mentioning the end of the credits where it says that Disney doesn't believe that all men pick their noses and that they don't hold the opinions of Kristoff, or whatever, and we both start cackling even harder."

"Wait," Riaz interjects. "Does it really say that?"

"Yes," I pronounce enthusiastically. "We didn't see it the first dozen times we watched the movie, but one night we were talking through the credits instead of fast forwarding to the post credit scene, and there it was. We paused it, read it a few times, and full on howled for ten minutes or so. We may have had a bit of wine, so we were particularly amused."

"That's funny. I'll have to look for it next time I watch it." Riaz writes another margin note to himself. I skip right over the part where he just admitted to watching a kid's movie and continue.

"Anyway, we were very in sync this particular day, and then I remembered that I hadn't told her about Christopher. Everything was suddenly dark and painful because I knew I had to tell her, but then she took the pause in conversation as an opening.

"'So guess what!' She was really excited, so I didn't want to burst her bubble.

"'What?' I said, remembering too slowly that on this day she told me her big news. I wanted to say, 'Wait, I have something you have to know right now!' but it was too late in so many ways.

"She clasped her hands together and, with a huge smile, said, 'I'm pregnant!'"

I shake my head, looking up at the stained, age-yellowed drop ceiling tiles above me.

"I hadn't told her yet. I hadn't told her about Christopher and the bimbo. And now I didn't know what to do. She was so happy, and I just wanted to scream. But, in a weird way, I was happy for her, too. The father might be an asshole, but she was getting to be a mom. She was making a family. Literally. So, I grabbed her hands and squealed, like I would have under any other circumstances, and we both stood and hugged and jumped up and down. All the while, I'm dying inside because I know what happened, what happens. Everything.

"Then I slipped back. I could feel it coming, too, so I hugged her harder and then was pulled away, back to the hospital room, with two nurses looking a little concerned, but not overly so. So I thought, at that moment, maybe the lapses were starting to get better. It was so much easier that time – I felt it coming, I felt it going, and I was okay. Little did I know, I was still on the roller coaster. It had just hit a straight patch."

Riaz shakes his head. "So you didn't tell her?" He looks incredulous.

"Hang on, now! I was put in an awkward position."

He groans. "Why didn't you call her or email her or text her the second you found out about him?"

"Because I thought it would be better in person, okay!" I sigh. "You don't think I feel bad about it? If I had told her before then, or if I could have told her that day, maybe things would have ended differently."

"So Christopher just gets away with it?" Riaz is starting to get really irritated. "He should suffer! He should be thrown out into the cold and flogged and tarred and feathered! He's such a cock-up, rubbish plonker!"

"Whoa!" I throw my hands up to calm him. "Slow your roll, Brit. Don't get your knickers in a twist. You're getting a little too into this story." Then I remember that he went to watch *The Princess Bride* and try to break the tension with a line from it. "Christopher doesn't get eaten by the eels at this time."

Riaz chuckles with recognition. "Shame," he says, shaking his head. "I'm just gutted for Sydney. That nutter's life should be in shambles."

I'm smiling back broadly, just like the day we met.

"What?" Riaz looks me over suspiciously.

"I didn't know how British you got when you were irritated."

He shakes his head. "An emotional response, I'm sure."

He sits up in his chair a bit, taking on an air of formality. "It's a bloody shame this chap wasn't held to account. He should have to pay his dues." He relaxes a bit, sitting back in his chair. "I just really hate injustice, bloody wanker." He emphasizes his accent heavily at the end.

"Well, you and me both. Maybe someday he will 'pay his dues.' Karma is tricky like that."

"So you don't know what happened to him?" Riaz looks surprised.

I shrug. "I haven't seen him since the night of the accident."

Riaz suddenly closes his eyes and hangs his head. "Of course. You would have had no reason to see him again. And…" – he evaluates me carefully before continuing – "…the baby?"

I shake my head, choking back the pain. "She hadn't yet been born."

Riaz's eyes moisten and he takes a hard swallow after a second. "I'm so sorry."

"Me, too." I let the tears flow.

Riaz stands and walks out of the room, returning with a box of tissues. He takes one and hands me the box. He dabs his eyes and takes a small step back.

"It's a tragic story. All of it. Terribly sad. But I wonder if holding onto all of this anger and pain is triggering the lapses. We already know that emotion seems to accelerate the process. Maybe, in time, you can learn to control the lapses by forgiving and forgetting. Holding on could just be exacerbating the feelings."

I shake my head. "Hate is a strong emotion."

"That's kind of my point." He sits and leans in towards me. "I don't want to see him ruin your life as well. Beyond the damage he has already done. Holding on to this hate and anger is slowly killing you."

"You're not being metaphorical, are you?" I ask, hugging myself with a sudden chill.

"I worry that, to keep you alive, we might have to engage in more active emotional maintenance. If you can find a way to release some of the emotional baggage you are carrying around, maybe you can prevent us from having to intervene."

"You're talking about medicating me."

Riaz nods.

"To remove my emotions?" I can hear the panic in my voice as it cracks a little. I pull out another tissue as I start crying from fear instead of sadness.

"Not remove, just meter," Riaz corrects, but his expression is not comforting. "It would keep you from experiencing extreme lows…" He trails off.

"Or extreme highs." I finish the thought. "You never met Sydney. You never met Christopher. You've only ever learned about them from what I've told you."

Riaz shrugs and lightly shakes his head, confused. "Yes, and?"

"Could you forgive him?"

Riaz looks a little shocked, his eyes widening. Then he sighs and furrows his brow. "No."

"You see my dilemma."

- 18 -

FIRE

Riaz holds my hand and runs his free hand through his hair, something I've seen him do when he doesn't know what else to say. He is about to say something, but I hold up my other hand and cut him off.

"What is it?" he asks, his expression quickly growing to concern when he looks into my eyes.

"It's happening."

It's all I can manage to say before I feel the pull of the lapse. I see Riaz stand and shove the chair against the wall with a single thrust and call out to the nurse's station, but then he is gone and I am blinking the stinging, acrid air of smoke out of my eyes and staring into a dark sky.

"You better move out of the smoke, kiddo!"

I immediately start to cry, afraid to turn, afraid I am wrong about the voice. This can't be happening.

Then Sydney dances across the yard in front of me, her sparkler leaving a trail of light behind her for a split second. I take in the scene, the smell of burgers and hot dogs on the grill, the fire pit in the middle of the yard, the hot summer air fading into the cooler evening. I shiver, but I'm not sure if it's because of the lapse or the chill. I am already pretty close to the fire pit, so I should be warm enough, but I'm still shaking.

I slowly turn to face my father, smiling behind his glasses as he pokes at the burgers with his tongs and drinks a beer. He looks at me and sees my eyes watering.

"Hey, Taylor May!" he exclaims with a deep chuckle, using my childhood nickname. "You're right in the stream of it! Seriously, you better move out of the smoke!"

He starts to try and loop the handle of the tongs onto a holder on the side of the grill but fails. I cough out a sob of sheer joy, seeing him do this again, like he did on every Fourth of July. Trying to be a grill master when he can't even get his tools to stay on their designated hooks.

"I'll get it," comes another voice, also tinged with amusement. I turn towards the voice, a new wave of tears streaming from my eyes. I can barely make her out through the deluge, but I reach my arms out instinctively.

"Mama?!"

She wraps her arms around me and effortlessly pulls me into the air and out of the smoke. "What were you doing, silly? Standing in the smoke like a little dragon?"

I giggle. I am suddenly aware that I am very young and everything seems okay. The trials of the future – of heartbreak and triumph and anger and too many funerals – all seem like a distant dream. I like that she calls me her little dragon and I make claws with my fingers and growl at her.

She laughs and feigns being afraid. "Oh no! My little dragon is going to eat me up!"

I throw my arms around her neck. "No, Mama," I hear myself say. "You're my dragon!"

"Well, of course I am!" She hikes me onto her hip and makes a claw with her free hand, growling with me. She smells like her roses and campfire.

But something is wrong. I don't want to think about it, but I know it. I push myself away from her chest and she sets me down, returning to the picnic table to do whatever she needs to do.

Something happens today. But what?

I start to walk around the yard. Something is so familiar.

"Syd!" I run over to her when I see what she's doing.

She has lit a new sparkler and is spinning around like a ballerina. "Dance with me!" she says in a voice like a princess. I start to spin with her, giggling as I get dizzy.

I hear a whine and stop spinning to investigate. Rusty, my wonderful golden retriever, is whimpering, trying to get closer to me, but he is clipped to a long leash tied around the tree. I race over to him and throw my arms around his neck, relishing the sloppy licks all over my face.

"Don't let him lick your face!" my mother is pleading. "He'll get you all slobbery!"

"I love slobber!" I say, reaching for the leash clasp.

"No, no!" my dad calls quickly. "Don't forget, we don't want him to get too near the fire!"

The fire.

How could I forget? I turn quickly, trying to locate Sydney, and I see that she's still spinning but getting wobbly. Rusty is still trying to lick me, but I push him away and start to run. I know now what is about to happen, I have to save my sister. I look down to my bare arms, unscathed and young and my breath catches for a second in my chest. But it doesn't matter.

Sydney, squealing with glee, spins once more, too close to the fire, and as she starts to trip, I shove her away from it, just like I did the day I was forever scarred. I know I will survive, though I'll be in the ICU for days. But if I hadn't reacted that evening, Sydney might not have survived. She was heading into the fire headfirst.

I know I'm about to fall into the fire pit and I won't be able to get out. When I catch myself on my arm, my weight will shove me down into the burning coals. I remember the smell of burning skin and hair, remember the agony that lasted for days and then the recovery, which took weeks.

I don't care what I did back then. The second I shove Sydney out of the fire, I plant my foot as hard as I can and launch myself with all the strength I can muster across the fire instead of into it. I can't endure that pain again. I won't. I scream in terror anyway, expecting the blistering heat.

Sydney is crying, like she understands what has just happened and that I saved her. My mother is screaming and dragging me by the arm away from the fire. My father tosses the last two beers out of his bucket of ice and throws its freezing water onto my legs.

I'm waiting for the sting of the burn to set in. The space around the worst of it should be screaming in pain, and I wonder why he threw the water on my legs instead of my arm, but I am clenching my teeth and squeezing my eyes shut, knowing what is about to come.

Only it doesn't.

My mother is looking me up and down, pulling the burned hem of my dress away from my legs while my father runs into the house, shouting about the first aid kit. Sydney is crouching on the ground, hugging her knees and swaying back and forth, whispering, "I'm sorry, I'm sorry," between sobs. She is biting her lip in her nervous way and I can't help but wonder if this is where that habit started.

My dad picks me up and sets me on the picnic table, a tube of burn cream in his hand. "I have the stuff. What should I do?"

My mom continues checking me over, finally grabbing my head and pulling it to her chest. "She's okay. Oh thank god."

"Are you sure? Her dress is burned straight through." Daddy starts exploring my legs for wounds.

"I know, I know, I saw that, too. But there aren't any burns. She's okay."

"My arm," is all I can gasp.

My mom pulls away, grabbing me by the wrists and turning my arms over, looking from side to side. After a second of panicked evaluation, she shakes her head towards my dad. Kindly looking back at me, she asks, "Is it your shoulder? You fell pretty hard!"

I stare down at my left forearm. The stinging pain is only in my mind. A memory of something that didn't happen. No. A memory that did happen that has now *changed*. "This is impossible," I whisper.

"I'd call it lucky as hell." My dad sighs out of relief.

"Language," my mom says automatically, though she's not really listening to him. "Sweetheart. You are okay." She takes my chin in her hand and tilts my face up to look at hers. "You were amazing. My strong, brave, and thankfully agile little dragon."

Sydney is still crying, but through deep sobs and sniffles, she manages to ask, "Is she okay?"

My mom smiles first at me and then at Syd. "She's fine. And, thanks to her, you are both fine."

I look between my sister and my arm several times. "Thanks to me, we are both fine," I repeat in complete disbelief.

- 19 -

SMOKE

I'm still staring down at my arm when the pull takes me out of the past and throws me violently into the future. That is, the present.

Riaz is barking orders to the nurses; one of them has a syringe poised beneath a bottle of something. She pulls the needle out of the bottle, squeezes the plunger a bit, and then injects the liquid into my IV. I can hear the alarms beeping wildly until Dr. Strove comes in, with a handful of ice packs, and directs one of the nurses to turn them off.

He starts hastily packing the ice around my body. It's bracing and I take a quick gasp.

"Taylor!" Dr. Strove is the first to see my eyes are open. He crosses to the opposite side of the bed from Riaz, placing his now cold fingers on my wrist and glancing up at the clock. Riaz gently places his hand under my head and tilts it towards him. He is shining a pen light in my eyes as I try to blink and push away the ice and Strove and Riaz.

"Please, Taylor, look here for me." He sounds so upset. Scared, even. I turn back towards Riaz, his hand gently cupping my chin now. I fight against the urge to squeeze my eyelids shut.

"Okay," he sighs. His hand lingers on my cheek for a second and then he brushes an errant lock of hair behind my ear, his thumb caressing my cheek as he does it.

My eyes instinctually flicker to Dr. Strove, who has seen the gesture and is now looking the two of us over with a furrowed brow.

"Sorry for the fuss, Doc," I manage to say to Strove, trying to remind Riaz where he is and who else is in the room. I'm suddenly aware that I'm a grown woman, not a child.

Riaz takes the hint and quickly retracts his hand.

"I've always thought you were a bit icy, Doc, but this seems a little over the top, doesn't it?"

Dr. Strove takes a thermometer out of a rolling tower of vital sign measuring tools. He sticks it into a dispenser with plastic covers and pulls the coiled cord loose, sticking the now sterile metal bit under my tongue.

"I think I'm okay," I try to say, but he shakes his head and gives me a kind smile.

"No jokes while I take your temperature, alright?"

I nod.

"No nodding," the thermometer beeps before I can gesture again anyway.

"Okay," he says, as he removes the plastic cover and returns the thermometer to the tower. "I just want to get that temperature down a little more." He turns to Riaz. "Dr. Choudhury, a word?"

"Of course." Riaz holds his breath for a brief second, but his expression remains unchanged.

Dr. Strove leaves first with most of the nurses. Riaz looks like he is steeling himself for a tough conversation. He sees me trying to push away some of the ice and says, "Leave those for a minute, okay? You were burning up."

He turns and leaves.

I was burning up. *The fire.* I pull up my left arm, several ice packs falling to the floor. Aside from some red marks where the ice had been right against bare skin, my arm is unscathed. It is completely fine.

This is impossible.

* * * *

Tears well up in my eyes as I feel my smooth skin. I'm panicking, breathing shallowly and trembling all over. Just outside my door I see Dr. Strove and Riaz having a heated discussion, Riaz putting his hands up defensively for a moment; Dr. Strove shakes his head and says one more thing before walking away.

Riaz runs a hand through his hair and then turns to look at me. When he sees my face, he briefly glances where Strove has gone and then comes to my side.

"You okay?" He observes my trembling and pulls some of the ice away. "That should help."

When he looks at me again, I can barely breathe. I can't speak.

"What is it?" He looks more anxious, glances at the machines and frowns, clearly troubled. "Damn!" He angrily smacks the nearest monitor. He reaches towards a button on the machine, but hesitates.

"What is it? I need you to talk to me. Your pulse is racing and your blood pressure is getting dangerously high. The nurses turned the damn alarms off. What is going on?"

He grabs my hands and leans down over the bed a little. "Please, talk to me!"

The bit of desperation in his voice and his tightening grip forces me to swallow hard and blink away my tears. "My burn. My scar…" I lift up my left arm to show him, waiting for his shocked response.

He gently grabs my arm and runs a finger over the red marks from the ice then sighs heavily. "The ice hasn't burned you. You should feel normal in a few minutes."

He starts to take away the other ice packs as I look around in disbelief. Had he forgotten?

"No," I shake my head. "My burn is gone!"

He places the ice packs on a tray that has been wheeled in and looks back at me questioningly. "What burn?"

"No, no, no!" I am sobbing. *What is happening? How could he not remember?* "No, the burn I got as a kid. The one from the lapse."

He nods, seemingly starting to understand. "You were burned in your lapse?"

"Yes," I say, wiping salty streams off my face.

"And you feel like it is still burning you?"

"No!" I can't think straight. "It left a scar. Don't you remember the scar?"

Riaz looks back at the arm. "It seems like the scar healed nicely. There's no trace of it."

"No, it never healed. My arm has been scarred since then. For most of my life! My arm was barely saved!"

Riaz looks back to the monitors and places his hands on my shoulders. I am shaking more now. "Okay, I believe you. I don't see a scar now, but you were burned as a little girl. I understand."

But he doesn't understand. He doesn't see that where I used to have an arm covered in scar tissue – just this morning! – raw, gnarled scar tissue, now I have nothing but smooth skin. He doesn't understand that my actions in the lapse changed my past.

I changed my past.

- 20 -

TREATMENT

Things have gone downhill. I've tried several times to explain everything to Riaz. At first, I thought he was just having trouble understanding what I was saying, but after the third or fourth attempt, I could see he was trying to handle me.

He doesn't believe me. He didn't believe me when I reminded him of our conversation about The Rookery in *The Name of the Wind*, though he was somewhat surprised that I knew he liked the book. He doesn't remember it, so in his mind I made the whole thing up. Since there is a problem with my brain, I can't be trusted, right? Nothing I am saying can be real. But *it is* real, and I need him to believe me.

* * * *

Riaz comes up to the door and knocks three times, gently.

I hate when he comes now. He looks at me differently, treats me like I'm a wounded bird trying to fly without knowing my wings have been broken. It's as if he keeps catching me and putting me back in the cage, only the cage is this facility, and if he would just let me go, back into a lapse, I could fly. I could change everything.

I am stronger than I was during the last lapse and all of my vital signs are back to normal. I try to be charming, try to make him feel that I am whole and of sound mind, but I'm afraid it comes off as cold and distant. I think I'm trying to handle him as much as he is me.

"How are you doing this morning?" he asks with a half-smile.

"Doing well," I lie, forcing a one-upping grimace in return.

"Great." He takes a tentative step in, looks at the monitors.

As he reaches towards my wrist I flinch. He seems wounded, but retracts his hand. "I can check that later," he says kindly.

"You had said I could go and see Carrie. I would like to do that, please." I find it hard to even look him in the eye. I feel so betrayed.

He looks at me for a second, then purses his lips together. "Sure. I don't see a problem with that."

"Great." I swing my legs over the side of the bed.

"Well, not at this moment." He puts up a hand.

"Why not?"

"Can I at least tell her you would like to see her, first?" He wraps both arms around his files and holds them to his chest like a shield. But despite this defensive gesture, he is raising his eyebrows at me and smiling.

"Right. Of course." I stay on the edge of the bed. "I'll wait here."

His face sinks a bit, but he quickly regains his composure. "I'll be right back."

* * * *

When he does return I am fully out of bed. I've traded the thin gown for sweatpants, a t-shirt, and a hoodie. The floor is cold on my bare feet, but I find that preferable to the weight of stiff sheets and thin blankets. I love having my skin touching the air.

"Right this way, miss." Riaz gestures out into the hall like a doorman at a fancy hotel. I shove my hands into the pockets of the hoodie and walk into the hall.

He leads me down the hall towards a wing of rooms I don't normally see and knocks three times on the doorframe of one of them, poking his head in. I don't hear a response, but he gestures towards the door and sends me in.

"Let me know if you guys need anything," Riaz says, almost as an afterthought, while walking out.

Carrie looks sunken and small, but her broad grin is the same. She has oxygen attached to her nose and as many wires and monitors as I do on my worst days.

"Hey, kid," she says quietly, but warmly.

I grab a chair along the wall and pull it to her bedside. "Hey, old lady."

She snorts a bit of a laugh and then coughs weakly for a few seconds. "Ah, this sucks. I'm sorry you have to see me like this, but I'm afraid it's this or nothing now."

A chill goes down my spine. "What do you mean?" I can feel a lump growing in my throat.

Carrie shakes her head and swipes at the air as if to tell me it's not worth crying over. "This is life, kid. You do your best, and then, you have to fold your hand."

I manage to keep my breath steady despite the streams of tears. I sniffle a little. "So, you're folding, huh? That's not like you."

"True," she grins. "True, true."

"So, what's going on?"

"Well, I suppose I have to tell you now." She sighs and takes my hand with one of hers, an IV line coming out of the thin skin of the back of her hand, taped in for the long haul. "I'm dying. I have been dying since before I met you."

I try to just listen, despite my growing sadness and fear.

"Stage four lung cancer. I was in another facility when Strove asked if I would be willing to come here and work with a patient of his that was having some trouble."

I snort a little. "Some trouble?"

"That's what I thought when I met you. Some trouble? Good god, this girl's a disaster! What have I gotten myself into?"

I laugh despite myself and that makes her smile.

"But then I got to know you and I am so happy that I did."

I can't stop the lurching sob as I bring her hand to my forehead and clutch her skin against mine.

"It's okay, kid. I'm comfortable for now, just not going to be a very good companion or card player."

"You could never be a bad companion," I smile. "Or card player."

"Well, you make it easy. You're terrible at cards."

"Hey!" I faux protest. "I should have taught you Exploding Kittens or even Zombie Dice. I could have destroyed you."

She shakes her head. "What is it with your generation? Everything is so apocalyptic."

"Melting icebergs, civil war, global pandemics, politicians in general," I offer, ticking each off on a finger.

"Alright, alright. Hard to argue with all that."

I lean forward. "Of course, I don't have any of those games with me, so we are stuck with gin rummy."

She chuckles, just a little, but it warms me.

"So what the hell have you been doing?" she asks. "I've been waiting for a visitor for weeks now."

"Weeks?" I repeat with a hint of disbelief. "What about Strove?"

"I think we both know he doesn't count in here."

"Has he started calling you Ms. Griffin every time he sees you?" I lean back and cross my arms.

"He wouldn't dare." She swats at the air in front of her like she is brushing the idea away. She turns her full attention back to me. "So spill it. What's going on with you?"

"Oh, you know," I sigh. "Lapsing and going into cardiac arrest and getting better and lapsing again."

"Again?" she says with concern.

"Yeah, once more, just as I was getting over the last one."

She looks thoughtful. "Those are getting pretty frequent."

"Yes," I say, looking at my hands in my lap.

"I don't know much about your lapses, but this sounds not great."

"That's putting it lightly," I commiserate. "But yeah, things are getting worse."

"Things?"

I look up at her. She has that knowing look on her face. She can understand that I'm talking about more than just the lapses.

"I can't sneak anything past you, can I?"

"Honey, you can't sneak anything past anybody. Judging from Riaz's pitiful exit just now, you two are on the outs?"

I raise an eyebrow but keep my head down. "He has decided to see me as more of a patient than a person."

She rubs her chin thoughtfully. "While I imagine that is for the best in the long run, I am curious as to why he would change his demeanor overnight."

"More like over-lapse," I say.

She tilts her bed up with a control lying near her right hand. The noise of the motor and sudden movement startle me a little and I look up at her. She is now sitting more upright and she feels more like the Carrie I know. "Explain."

I sigh. "Something happened. I just…" I'm having trouble finding the words. "I just realized that the lapses are more than brain chemistry issues."

She nods, but her brow has furrowed, which always makes me feel I'm about to be scolded. "What do you mean? What did you do? You told the brain expert that he didn't know what was happening in your brain?"

"When you put it like that…" I cringe a little. "But yes, I guess. I tried to explain that the lapses weren't hallucinations or delusions or any of that."

"So, what are they then?"

"You wouldn't believe me if I told you."

"Try me," she says, with a look of staunch determination.

"It's a long story."

"I have nothing but time, girl. Just not a lot of it, so get going."

* * * *

Carrie stares at me with more than a little disbelief. "That is a hell of a story."

"I told you that you wouldn't believe me." I lean back again and hug my arms. I'd been leaning forward for at least an hour, trying to tell her a short version of my strange tale of the fire.

"I believe that you believe it."

I shake my head. "That is exactly the problem." I throw my hands in the air.

"How so?"

"I don't want you to believe that I believe it. That means that you also believe I'm losing my mind, or crazy, or delusional, or something else awful."

"Hmmm," she starts, crossing her arms. She thinks for a moment. "Okay, let's say, for the sake of argument, that I do believe you. How would that be any different? I can't help you with Riaz or Strove, I can't get you released from here. What benefit do you get if I am on your side with this, frankly, hard-to-swallow premise?"

"An ally, for one," I say, feeling the weight of the truth being lifted slightly with the hope of being able to share it. "And, I don't know, maybe you can help me figure this out."

She shrugs. "Allies are nice. But, honestly, kiddo, figure what out?"

"I need to figure out this whole thing. Figure out why the lapses happen, why I go back to certain memories or times or whatever, and figure out how I can be less of a passenger and more of a driver."

"Driver? Meaning you want to control your lapses."

"Not control so much as steer. If what I am saying is true, if I can really enter a lapse and change something, if I can alter my own past, then that means…"

"You can change other pasts as well," she finishes with a shocked expression.

"If I can change the past, I can change *her* past," I continue, again leaning towards her. "I can get my sister back."

- 21 -

RECORDS

I still think Carrie doesn't believe me, but she isn't one to give up on a challenge. I'm allowed to visit her for an hour twice a day – once in mid-morning and once in the afternoon. Dr. Strove wants to cut that down to preserve her strength and health, but both Carrie and I have argued that we need each other, and he lets us continue.

Carrie's room has become HQ to the project of figuring out what is causing my lapses. Every day I bring my journal and as much loose paper as I can coax Strove or Riaz to give me or I can sneak from the nurses' station.

We have two goals – the first is to continue to document my lapses in my journal, with as much detail as I can remember. Riaz still takes the journal every once in a while, and looks through the notes. I'm sure he relates what he reads to Strove, so we're careful not to put in any details that will make them think I'm becoming more delusional, which is their current theory.

Our second goal is to document theories – as many concepts as we can think of, no matter how outlandish. We are brainstorming ways to try and figure out how to control, or "steer" as I like to say, the lapses in a direction to change the bits of my past that could affect Sydney.

When one of the nurses or Strove or Riaz casually walks by, Carrie makes sure we are talking about the lapses as if working through them for my benefit. Since Riaz has already heard most of the story, the staff seems content that I'm only relaying the same information to my friend.

When we are certain no one is around, however, I pull out the loose pieces of paper from under her thin mattress and we create diagrams and timelines and theories.

In the past few days, I have caught her up to the point where I had explained everything to Riaz – up until the lapse where I relived the time I found out Christopher was cheating on Syd.

"When did that happen, in real history?" Carrie is writing notes on a clipboard she got from Strove, her eyes focusing intently on whatever she has written.

"It was sometime in spring of last year. They hadn't even been married a whole year. He's such an asshole."

"We can agree on that. But, can you be more specific?"

"About his asshole-ness?"

Carrie gives me a look. "No, about the date, at least the month."

I sigh heavily and puff out my cheeks as I think. "Hmmm. I was returning her gardening equipment, which means I had just planted my spring flowers for my deck."

"So that would be, what, April?"

I grimace. "It would be April if I were timely, but I'm usually not. So, I would guess more like May. Mid-May, more likely."

She frantically scribbles something on her paper. "Okay, and the wedding was in August two years ago, right?"

"Yes, August twentieth."

"Okay, okay. Can you remember any other specific dates?"

I shrug. "Um, I can tell you that the crash was on October 12th last year, the first lapse was in the hospital, one or two days after that. Honestly, we would need my medical file to find out when the lapses all were."

"That's it!" Carrie slams the clipboard down into her lap. "Those will be specific dates and times, then we can try to work back to see if there are any patterns."

Her plan is starting to become clear to me. "True, but I doubt they'd let me see what they're putting in my medical file. They are all smiles and nods, but undoubtedly the notes are 'patient goes crazy' and stuff like that."

Carrie laughs, then her coughing starts again. This is a fairly regular occurrence now. She is growing weaker, and each time the coughing starts, our brainstorming sessions are abruptly cut short. She quickly hands me the clipboard and pencil and I gather up any other loose papers and step away from the bed. This is the routine. We hide our work and then I slip out while the nurses tend to her. Before I can get the last few pages this time, Carrie grabs my wrist, looking to the door before any of the staff can come in. "You need to get that file."

"How?" I whisper back, looking over my shoulder.

"Try making a friend," she manages to say before the coughing takes over again.

She lets me go as the nurses come in, pushing my chair away from her bedside and shooing me out the door.

With the flair of a conspirator, I faux salute her with two fingers as I enter the hall, tucking the loose papers under my hoodie. How the hell am I supposed to make a friend that can help me with this? I can barely make friends as it is. I slowly make my way back to my room. I'm slow mostly to keep the papers from rustling and notifying all the staff that I'm hiding something, but I'm also just not in a hurry to get back to my room. I dread the long hours of solitude now that my time with Carrie is restricted and Riaz has been keeping his distance.

As I pass the nurse's station, Nurse Now-Orange-Nails looks up from her desk and calls to me. "The doctor would like to see anything you've come up with in that..." – she hastily points to the journal – "book of yours."

I nod and hand it to her. I start to continue on, but Carrie's voice in my head urges me to stop. I turn back to her. "Hey, so, what's your name?"

She sits up in her chair and sets her hands on her hips. "You seriously don't know my name?"

I shake my head, chastised. "But you've been here the longest, and you're one of the only faces I know, and I feel I should know your name, too. If that's okay."

Her posture relaxes a bit. "I'm Dominique," she says after a pause.

"Dominique." I roll the name around in my mouth. "That's a beautiful name."

"Thank you," she says with a hint of skepticism.

I feel like I am already blowing it.

"Sure," I say, turning towards my room. "I'm Taylor, by the way."

"I know," she says, slightly insulted.

"Right." I decide to leave before I end up insulting her any further, but I'm a split second too slow.

"Out of curiosity," she starts, and I turn back towards her quickly, "What do you call me when you're talking to your friend, the old lady? I must have come up in some conversation."

My cheeks pink up and my eyes are wide. "We call you Nurse Orange-Nails."

Her eyes flick down to her nails, which she has extended out in front of her as if verifying the color. "They aren't always orange."

"No," I add hastily. "They aren't, but we refer to you by whatever color they are that day. Green, purple, sparkly. Your New Year's Eve nails were spectacular, by the way."

This elicits an excited expression. "Thank you! I was proud of those."

"You do them yourself?" I say with honest admiration.

"Of course I do. You think I'm going to get a manicure every five days? This job does not provide for luxuries like that."

I smile. "Of course not. You just get to deal with headaches like me." I shrug. "Sorry about that."

She purses her lips together, but she doesn't seem upset. "You're not that bad, so long as you keep your head on straight." She extends a finger in my direction and makes a little gesture motioning to all of me.

"Right," I say with a quick acknowledgement. "I'll do my best."

"That's all any of us can do." She shrugs and turns her attention back to a stack of papers on her desk.

"It's nice to meet you, Dominique." I contentedly head towards my room.

"You, too," comes her reply after a second – a gesture that warms me to my core.

* * * *

I wait until there is no one nearby and shove the loose papers under my mattress. This feels risky, as my bed is stripped and remade when I leave the room, whereas Carrie's has to be changed around her, making hers a safer storage location. But, I have no choice.

After I stash the papers I feel suddenly sneaky and hurry out of my room. Without Carrie to go to, I wander until I come to the game room. The cards on the shelf make me miss my time with Carrie more, so I ignore them and instead pull a chair to the window to watch Office Building TV.

It's been so long, I have no idea what to expect. Scruffy and Manager Lady are still there, but Headphones Guy seems to have moved on and the empty cubicle next to him now has an older woman in what appears to be a too-tight pant suit diligently typing on a new computer. She has put up photographs, which of course I can't see clearly from here, and an old-school wall calendar, which feels wonderfully nostalgic.

I tip back slightly, putting my feet up on the sill and wait for something to happen. Carrie was right, I'm always waiting for something to happen instead of gripping my opportunities.

How in the hell am I supposed to get access to my medical file?

Your mission, should you choose to accept it, I think, *Mission Impossible* coming to mind, *is to find a way to snatch your medical file and read all the little details that you will instantly regret knowing. This message will self-destruct in five seconds.*

I shake my head to myself. "Too soon," I whisper, realizing that the message is in my head, and therefore more a comment on my mental health than my mission.

"Too soon for what?"

My shoulders tense at the sound of Riaz's voice, but I try to relax, turning my head slightly towards him. "Too soon to judge the new office worker," I lie.

Riaz pulls a chair beside me and sits, his forearms resting on his thighs as he peers out the window.

"The woman to the right of your Cubies, or the one up a couple of floors?" he asks.

I strain to look up at the higher window. The reflection of the sun is hitting me right in the eyes and all I can make out is a hand against the glass before my head flashes in pain from the brightness. "I meant the Cubie. I can't see the other person. The light is blinding at this time of day and he or she has their hand on the glass." I lean back out of the light. "They can probably see us better than we can see them."

"She," he says, leaning forward and squinting.

"Why do you say that?"

"Her hand is more…"

My eyebrows arch. "Yes?"

"More…"

"Delicate, feminine, petite?" I offer.

"No, more graceful. Her fingers look like ballet dancers. I don't know many guys with graceful fingers. She has fingers like yours."

I now resent when I can feel my cheeks warming when he says something that can be perceived as a compliment. "You think my fingers are like ballet dancers?"

"Yes," he says, matter-of-factly. "Especially when you draw."

"You've seen me draw?" I lean forward a little to look around at his face.

"I may have seen you drawing. Once or twice. From a distance."

I lean back with a thud, but I'm smiling. "Creeper."

He snorts a little.

The pause in conversation has weight. I can't stand it. "Anyway, yes. It's too soon to judge Pant Suit."

"That's not a flattering name."

I shrug. "I didn't make her wear it."

There is an awkward silence between us.

His head drops a little. "I'm sorry," he whispers.

I try to think of a joke, but all I can do is breathe past the lump in my throat.

"You deserve more," he says. "Deserve to be healed, but I don't know what is happening to you or how I can help."

I know how you can help, I think to myself, trying to devise a plan to wrangle my medical files.

He turns towards me but can't bring himself to look into my eyes. "I don't have any more ideas."

I realize that what he is actually saying is that he's giving up. He's apologizing because he is going to leave.

"Don't go," I blurt out before I can stop myself.

He sighs deeply and hangs his head. "I have no reason… " – he pauses – "no medical justification to stay."

"Stay for me," I mutter as tears form in my eyes, making everything blur slightly.

He shakes his head almost imperceptibly. "I can't."

I can barely hear the words.

"Screw it," I say with a sudden desperate conviction. "I need you."

He clasps his hands together hard, his knuckles turning white. "Please don't."

"I know this isn't convenient. I know it can't go anywhere and that coffee-at-a-café dream isn't going to happen. And I know you think I'm crazy, but I think I love you," I say, plunging ahead in a manic voice. "I know I do. You are gentle, kind, intelligent, and handsome. You are the most wonderful man I've ever met and I don't care that I'm a patient and you're a doctor and I'm probably dying. And I don't care about your ethics and your rules!" I pause, just for a second. "I mean, I do care about ethics and rules, I just think they suck. This sucks. This whole situation. I don't want to be here without you. This last week has been murder, with you treating me like a lost cause, Carrie dying, and Strove wanting to commit me. I know it sounds crazy, I know *I* sound crazy, but I would love you if I met you anywhere else, under any other circumstances, and I don't understand how I am supposed to just not feel because of our stupid circumstances."

He grabs my hand and I stop my tirade. "That's why I need to go."

I shake my head and yank my hand back. "Because I have gotten too attached."

"No," he says, forcefully taking both of my hands in his and looking me in the eye. "Because I have."

"Doctor," Dominique says gently at the doorway.

Riaz abruptly drops my hands and stands, leaving the room without another word. He rushes past Dominique, who looks after him with a scowl, and turns back to me with a softened expression. She retrieves his chair and sits next to me.

"It's so unethical —" she starts.

"Because I'm crazy and can't make those determinations for myself."

"No," she says a bit haughtily. "It's unethical that he should have gotten this attached to you, that's true, but not because you're crazy, which I definitely think you are. But, instead, because he can't treat you properly because he's in love with you."

I look at her in disbelief. "Yeah, right."

"Oh, please. You would have to be blind not to see how much that poor man is enamored with you."

"Say you're right. It's not enough." I shake my head.

"The best thing he can do for you, for the both of you, is let Strove figure you out and give you two a chance on the outside. He's just postponed that as long as he could because he does want to cure you. He doesn't want to give up on you."

"I'm about to lose everything all over again," I sob.

Dominique rubs her hand along my back. "You've still got Dr. Strove and the old lady."

"Who is dying," I remind her.

She squeezes my shoulder a little. "And you've got me, too."

It is nice to have someone else I can turn to. Carrie would be so proud of me. This girl-talk from Dominique is somewhat of a surprise, but she seems sincere.

"Can I ask you something?"

Dominique leans forward to see my face. "Sure, sugar."

"Do they know how much longer I have?"

She thinks for a long moment and then shakes her head. "You'd have to ask Dr. Strove. From what I understand, though, your episodes are getting worse and the damage to your body is becoming permanent."

"Wow. No one has told me that."

"All you have to do is ask." She places a reassuring hand on mine.

She seems genuinely concerned and helpful, so I take a risk. This opening in the conversation seems too good to pass up. "Do you think you could help me see my medical record?" I ask, bracing for rejection.

"Of course," she says.

I'm shocked. "What? Isn't it confidential or something?"

"Yes," she laughs. "It is confidential, from everyone who has no reason to see it without your permission. But it is *your* medical record."

"Really? I'm allowed to see it?"

"Yes." She shakes her head, astounded. "Did you think I'd have to steal it for you or something?"

I can't help but shrug. "I guess I did."

"And you thought we were close enough after a day of being friendly with each other for me to break the law on your behalf."

"I was hopeful," I admit, sheepishly pursing my lips together.

"Hmph," she snorts as she stands up. "Would you like me to bring it here to your perch in the game room window, or to your room, Super Spy?"

"Well now I feel like it needs to be a covert operation, so maybe a dead drop on the bookcase?" I joke.

She chuckles. "I'll be right back."

- 22 -

EMERGING PATTERNS

Medical records are no joke. Most of the printouts, files, images, data and jargon are a complete mystery to me. There are some details that are clear, like blood pressure and pulse rate, and explanations on some of the medical documentation is fairly comprehensible, but there is also a lot of information that I just can't interpret or understand.

But I'm not worried about the technical jargon. If that made some sort of diagnosis possible, the doctors would have figured it out. I'm only interested in dates.

I pore over the file for the next several hours, pulling out every date that I see and trying to correlate that with my memory of events. Aside from the actual dates and times of everything, there is not much else that I can glean from the files.

When I head back to Carrie the following day, I have a list of all of the lapses and how long they lasted based on the start and end times listed in the file. I know that some of the time entries are incorrect, because I was alone when the lapse began, but it is a starting place.

"I didn't realize you had that many lapses," Carrie muses as she looks over my data.

"I lost track, admittedly, but there you have it. Eleven lapses between October fourteenth of last year and March twelfth of this year."

"There doesn't seem to be any rhyme or reason," Carrie says distractedly. "The lapses happen in as little as three days and as many as seventeen. When was your last lapse?"

"Two weeks ago, Tuesday," I remind her.

"Right, the fifteenth." She rubs her eyes. "And why did you copy down the start and end times for each lapse?"

"Oh, Riaz thought the time duration of the lapse might correlate to the time of the actual past event. It was just something we were tossing around."

Carrie drops her hands and looks at me. "But that isn't how memory works."

"I know. We thought it was weird, too, which is why I wrote them down."

Carrie pulls out a new piece of paper and writes a column of dates on one side. "Okay, let's think about this. If the time of the lapse does correlate to the past, maybe it links to more."

"Meaning?" I lean towards her.

"I'm not sure yet. Let's be more methodical. Lapse one was on…" – she flips back to the other sheet of paper where I've written everything down – "October fourteenth. That is two days after the crash, and you went back to…" She looks up at me.

"Um, I went back to my sister's wedding. August twentieth, two years ago."

"Okay. The lapse was at five-fifteen in the evening. What time was your sister's wedding?"

I see where she's going with this. "She walked down the aisle at five-thirty, or, that was the plan. I didn't time it precisely, but the wedding planner was pretty solidly on it."

"Okay, so that lines up not only with duration, but time of day." Carrie has become invested and excited.

"Second lapse?" I urge her on.

"Lapse two was on October sixteenth and you went where?"

The fact that she is using terms of actual travel is freaking me out and kind of thrilling, too. "Second lapse I went to coffee with my sister. I don't know the date of that in reality, but it would have been after my friend Lucy's birthday, which is June fifteenth, and before Aaron moved in with me in the beginning of July."

"Okay, that gives us a window," Carrie says. "This lapse was at around one in the afternoon."

I can feel the blood draining from my head. "Yeah, that tracks," I whisper.

Carrie looks up at me. "Stay with me, kid. We're onto something real here."

I press my hands together and against my lips, as though praying for a real answer. "Riaz had wondered if there was this type of correlation, but I thought that was impossible." I feel so dumb that I dismissed the idea. We might have been able to determine more, together.

Carrie seems to read my thoughts. "Well, we're onto it now. Let's just move forward, okay?"

"Yep." I try and refocus, tuning out my clamoring thoughts.

We work our way through all the other lapses, marking down what I can remember without supporting information, and a pattern starts to emerge. Not only do the lapses match in duration, but in time of day. Every single lapse seems to happen at the same time as the past event. It has to mean something. But I can't remember enough detail about specific dates to determine if there is a larger pattern.

The excitement and exertion takes a lot out of Carrie, and I know that we are racing against time in more ways than one.

We continue working on this theory daily. After each of our sessions, which are becoming shorter and shorter, Dr. Strove or one of the nurses shoos me out of her room. I'm always excited to see her, because it really does feel like we are onto something, but I can see that she is deteriorating quickly. It's a fact I am actively ignoring.

In the midst of all of this, I'm trying to remember things more clearly, work up more data to share with Carrie, and convince all of the medical staff that I am perfectly well.

Riaz hasn't been back in a few days, but I can't stomach that he is gone for good. The thought alone makes me lightheaded and I can't afford another lapse, so I use every calming mechanism in my toolkit to stay levelheaded and in the present.

* * * *

I am eagerly waiting for the go-ahead to visit Carrie when I see Riaz from the corner of my eye walking towards the nurse's station.

I can't help but try and find out what he's up to, so I quietly walk over to where he's talking to Dominique. She is scowling at him slightly, but spots me coming up behind him and declares, loudly, "You should return it to her yourself. She's right there." She points at me and with that turns away from him and busies herself at the other side of the nurse's station.

Riaz retracts the journal he's been holding out towards her, his shoulders slumping slightly, and turns to see me.

"Hello," he says wearily. He looks tired and emotionally raw.

I can't hold my anger for him after seeing his pitiful expression, so I shove my hands in my pockets and reply, "Hey."

"How are you doing?"

"I'm okay."

"How is Ms. Griffin?"

I shake my head slightly. "She's getting worse. I'm thankful for the time we have together, though."

"That's good. You should spend as much time with her as you can." His eyes are sad and understanding.

"Are you headed there…," he continues, right as I say, "Are you leaving soon?"

"You first." He gestures to me with my journal.

"I was just asking if you were leaving already."

He affirms this with one small bow of his head. "In a couple of days. I'm just trying to wrap up and help Strove with your treatment plan."

"Right." I swallow hard. "Thanks."

This uncomfortable exchange is making me anxious. I try to change the subject.

"What were you going to say?"

"I was just asking if you were headed to see Ms. Griffin."

"Not yet. She needs her rest. Doctor's orders."

"Of course," he says.

"You know, you never heard the end of the story."

He looks at me curiously. "What do you mean?"

"I never told you the rest of the story. After Christopher cheated, what led up to the crash, what happened after the crash."

He shrugs. "I guess I just assumed an ending. And I know pretty much everything that happened after the accident."

"Do you?" I raise an eyebrow and manage a coy smile. "How much trouble would it really be to hear the last bit of my story?"

His expression softens, but then he looks over his shoulder towards Strove's office. "I really shouldn't."

"You'll regret it, once you leave," I try and tempt him. "Never knowing what really happened to all of these characters, all of the drama. Not knowing who got their dues, who suffered the most, what happens to everyone." I'm trying to lure him in, as if my life were one of the books we both like.

"I guess I only really cared about what happened to you." He moves to clasp his hands in front of him, which reminds him he is still holding my journal. He holds it out to me. "I think this belongs to you."

I reach out and take it, letting my fingers overlap his for a moment. "Your loss," I mutter. "I'll be in the game room, should you change your mind."

- 23 -

OLD PATTERNS

When Riaz comes into the game room several minutes later, I'm sitting at our usual table, shuffling cards so that I can play another game of solitaire while I wait to see Carrie.

He sits down and leans over the table, resting his elbows in a familiar way while lacing his fingers together. It's the same posture he would take while listening to me for all these weeks. It feels like we are falling into our old pattern.

"You have my undivided attention. I am actually desperate to know the end of the story," he admits.

"And that's okay with everyone?" I raise an eyebrow and shuffle the cards one more time.

"I'm leaving at the end of the week, consulting with Dr. Strove over the next few days. I think I can spare you an hour or two."

"I'm so flattered." I square up the deck and put it on the table. "So where were we?"

"Lapse number six, I believe."

"Right." I take a deep breath, then begin. "Lapse number six happened a couple of weeks later. We thought – that is Dr. Strove and I thought – maybe I was over the worst of it. I even asked him, and Strove confirmed that it was the longest I'd gone without a lapse. I had mostly worked through all of the emotions I'd had about the whole situation, so we were hopeful. Then, one night, I was overcome with grief. No real trigger, per se, just an onslaught of loss. A realization, I think, that there wasn't anything left for me outside the hospital."

"How do you mean?"

I almost chastise him for interrupting, but then I realize he doesn't know. "I had lost my job at this point, which is no great loss to be honest, but I had no family or friends either."

"Didn't you tell me once you had an uncle? He was at your sister's wedding, right? And what about Aaron?"

"I do have an uncle, somewhere, but we're not close. To be honest, I don't think I even have his contact information. Syd was the one who always tried to keep track of everyone.

"Aaron…" I bite the inside of my lip. "Aaron visited me once. In the hospital, after I found out about Syd, but before I was moved here. He told me he had been offered a job in Chicago, which is closer to his family. Since I wasn't able to help with bills, he had to give up the apartment. He told me it was okay, he had taken care of everything. He even saw to the arrangements for Syd's service, which I couldn't attend, of course."

"That's a lot for a friend to take on."

"It was. And I was grateful. But then I understood why he was really leaving. See, he loved Syd, had really fallen for her, and he was devastated. And he felt guilty. Guilty that he didn't tell her, didn't save her, didn't stop the wedding or whatever else he thought he could have done."

"Neither of you could have known, and neither of you could possibly be responsible."

"Nonetheless, it was more than he could take." I hang my head. "He packed up and stored my stuff, sublet the apartment, and moved away so he could forget."

"He abandoned you," Riaz whispers, realization in his eyes.

"Everyone does," I say. There is more accusation in my voice than I intend and Riaz apparently feels the sting, guilt spreading across his face.

"At any rate," I continue, "after Aaron's visit I realized I had nothing. No job, no apartment, no family, and no friends."

"My God," Riaz sighs.

"I was overwhelmed with desperation, and then I lapsed, and found myself shaking violently, but holding on to a bar top. When my head cleared, I found my nails had dug into the polyurethane. At first, I thought it was because of the lapse itself, but then I looked at my surroundings and there he was – Christopher, walking towards me. I remembered I was supposed to meet Aaron – go figure – but he wasn't there yet, and Chris had the nerve to walk right up to me.

"He had this sort of threatening glare and he pulled up a stool right next to me, looking around like he didn't want anyone to see us together, like it was some sort of clandestine meeting.

"I snapped at him. 'What the hell do you want?' I was seeing red. I don't even remember exactly what he told me, he just waffled between intimidating me and begging for another chance, explaining that he was going to be there for Syd and the baby, which made me so mad I full on slapped him."

"Brilliant job." Riaz leans towards me seriously. "Twit deserved that."

"He deserved a hell of a lot more, but yes. The bartender came over, looked at Chris hostilely and asked me if everything was okay. It took me a second to answer him, then I nodded before I got up in Christopher's face and told him if he didn't clean up his act I'd be sure he never saw either of them ever again.

"Of course, I have no idea how I would have made good on that threat, but I was really angry. I grabbed my bag and started to leave and he grabbed my wrist. Hard. And pulled me back so he could whisper in my ear that I'd regret threatening him. I pulled my wrist away, just as the bartender noticed and motioned for the bouncer to get Chris. Before that drama could start,

I stormed out of there. I had so much rage I basically powerwalked all the way back to the apartment, and when I threw open the door I started yelling at Aaron. Well, not at him, but yelling my frustration loudly towards him – but he stopped me really quickly. He was talking over me in a ridiculously loud voice; he had wide eyes and a forced smile.

"Then I saw that he was sitting on the couch, drinking wine with Syd. She looked a little guilty and embarrassed. I immediately shut up. I couldn't tell her about Christopher because I had lost that chance, or at least I felt I had. God, I should have said something. But, like the rest of this tragic tale, I didn't. She made some quick excuse to leave, gave me a hug, and rushed out the door.

"I was angry and a little hurt. I felt betrayed by Aaron, because he had stood me up to drink with my sister, and then I was mad that she was drinking, because she was pregnant. I sort of jumped down his throat, you know?"

"Sorry, no, what does that mean?"

"Oh," I start, surprised. "I mean I yelled at him. I started asking him what she was doing here, why he stood me up, why they were drinking together.

"He explained that nothing had happened, they were just hanging out. He calmed me down. Apparently, she had come by for the gardening equipment. I had failed to tell her that I returned it already because that would have meant having to decide whether to tell her what I saw when I was at her house. Aaron tried to convince me she hadn't been there very long, pointing out she hadn't even had a chance to drink her wine, and I realized that she hadn't been drinking after all and clearly also hadn't told Aaron she was pregnant.

"Funnily enough, this was the moment I also realized he had feelings for her. And I understood he did not have feelings for me, at least not the kind I wanted. It was also pretty clear that she thought of him as more than just a friend, Christopher or no Christopher. And I had missed my chance to tell her about Christopher and I didn't know how to tell Aaron anything, and I was just freaking out. Then I looked down at my wrist and it was starting to bruise a little and all of my jumbled emotions condensed into fury.

"It was all too much for me. It was all strong enough that I came through the violent lapse storm to end up back in the hospital, surrounded by nurses and Dr. Strove again. There was nothing I could do but kick myself again for not having done something to help her. I hadn't even told her about Chris grabbing me at the bar. It was like each lapse was showing me another opportunity that I could have helped her, and another time I let her down."

Riaz raises his hand slightly to stop me. "Do you really think that's what's happening?"

"I mean, it has crossed my mind."

"That could help us. Of course!" Riaz stands up, excited. "We need to handle the triggers more directly, stop them at the source." He starts to walk away. "I'm sorry, I have to talk to Dr. Strove. I will be back soon to hear the rest of the story, but maybe we *can* fix this. Maybe you really can tell me the rest over coffee at a café instead of stuck in here, huh? I have an idea. I finally have an idea." With that, he practically runs out of the game room.

"So much for keeping his interest," I say to no one in particular. If he really can help me, he might stop the lapses. But I can't let him do that.

- 24 -

HIDDEN

I try to go see Carrie, but when I get to her room one of the newer nurses shakes her head and closes the door in my face, Carrie shrugging weakly behind her.

I can't wrap my head around what Riaz meant by "handling the triggers directly." If he can figure out something to separate me from my lapses, from my memories, he would be separating me from my *actual* past.

Without Carrie to talk to, I can feel myself spiraling. Earlier, before meeting with Riaz, I took my wrist monitor off and gave it to Dominique to charge. She still hasn't brought it to me. She must have forgotten about it. I assume she left it somewhere out of sight, as I know right now it would be lighting up like an amusement park. I just need to avoid her, because she'll remember if she sees me. The other nurses don't pay much attention to me since I'm less of a hassle now, so as long as they don't see my naked wrist and I don't act strange, I should be able to get somewhere a little more private before I lapse.

Because I know I am about to lapse.

I'm aware that the episodes are becoming more dangerous, but if I don't try and control my own mind, drive the lapses, then Riaz and Strove will take away my only chance of saving Syd. I have to take the risk that I can calmly transition through the shift – just like I did the second time, when I lapsed to a coffee date with Syd. I know that I can do this without repercussions, but I can't do it if I am being monitored.

I'm trying to breathe slowly, distract myself from the inevitable collapse, stay calm, but everything is starting to blur. I know I won't make it all the way to my bed, so before I lose consciousness, I duck behind my door and try to slide down the wall. I don't know if I make it all the way down or not.

* * * *

My breath catches as I expect to hit the cold linoleum floor and am instead blinded by a bright, sunlit morning. The cars driving past, the bikes, the pedestrians, even the other café patrons are too much for me. The noise, the bustle, the light – for the first time I understand sensory overload.

I close my eyes and try to breathe more calmly, letting the ambient smells and sounds normalize for me while I give my eyes a second to adjust.

"I know, I know," Syd says, shaking her head. She must think I'm reacting to something she said rather than struggling to acclimate, attempting to stay calm.

"Know what?" I try to shake away my blurred vision and growing headache.

"I know you don't like Christopher, or at least you didn't when we first met him, but – "

I can't let her continue. My tranquility is shattered and with fury, I slam my hands on the table. "*Didn't* like him? Like that might change?" I am seething and Sydney sits upright, shocked.

"What on earth…?" she starts, but I shake my head.

"He is evil, and slimy, and a coward. He will hurt you, he has hurt you, hurt me, destroyed everything…" My head starts aching.

"Just try and stay calm." I look to my side and see the homeless man from this day staring right at me, his hands going out to steady me.

What? How is this possible?

My mind is racing. I can't put together everything that is happening with Syd, this man, my own brain. This doesn't usually happen. My thoughts are muddling.

I turn my attention back to Syd. "He gets you killed," I manage to say, but Syd doesn't hear me, she is frantically motioning to another patron, who whips her phone out as others start to come towards us. The pain is overwhelming. I think about the me in the future, alone on a cold floor with no monitors, and I can't help but scream in agony and terror. I may have just killed myself.

* * * *

The scream brings me to myself in a hospital bed. There are beeping monitors, hurrying nurses, and light streaming in through the windows. Despite the pounding headache I still have, I can tell this is not my room. This is not the facility at all.

"What...?" I am still blinking away the brightness, this room seems even worse than the café.

A comforting hand rests on my shoulder. "Don't you worry, you're safe and we are going to take care of you." I know the voice, but I can't place it. I take a deep breath to try and evaluate my surroundings despite the pain and brightness. It's Marnie. From the ICU. My breath catches.

"What day is – " I start, but I'm interrupted when she looks up and the ER doctor that treated me after the crash, Dr. Buchannan, walks in. He begins to check me over, anxiously it seems, using a penlight to look into my eyes, which is agonizing.

"How are you feeling?" he says. I am so baffled I cannot think, cannot comprehend what is happening, where I am, *when* I am.

"My head, it's killing me," I manage and he nods.

"I don't doubt it. You gave us quite a scare, Ms. Donlan."

"Taylor," I respond reflexively.

"Of course," he smiles. "Taylor. Well, we are definitely going to want to keep you for some more tests and observations. This habit of yours, of seizing unpredictably, is very concerning."

"Right." I remember. This whole scene is after the second lapse. After the lapse where I met Syd for coffee. Again. How am I here again?

"You were experiencing some dangerous symptoms," Dr. Buchannan begins.

I can feel it now. A constant within myself that grounds me. I am here, in the past, between coffee with my sister and my lapse in the future. I remember this conversation with Dr. Buchannan and I recite the words he said to me the first time I was here. "Hypertension, hyperthermia, seizing, and arrhythmia, right?"

He scowls, looking down into my medical file. "Yes, among other things. Has this happened to you before?"

I can only stare at him, as though he must be joking. But, of course he isn't, and at this time in my life I had only had one lapse.

"Have you had an episode like this before?" he asks again.

"Lapse," I correct him, the pain in my head worsening again.

"What was that?"

My body is shivering and I can feel my heart rate pound in my head. I still have the headache, which is making it hard to concentrate, but I can feel other parts of my body – my muscles, my lungs – lurching between the different timelines. It's as if my brain is stopping at a rest area on a chaotic freeway, trying to let every bit of me catch up before moving on.

"You kept me alive," I stutter, gasping as the pain increases again. "You are keeping me alive. Maybe they'll have time to find me."

Dr. Buchannan fades away, though I can see he is trying to ask me questions, looking to the nurses for medication, monitors, and equipment. I can't help but be thankful for them, for this horrible day, because without it, I'm sure I would have died in this transition. I just, impossibly, moved through three different timelines, and I just may survive them all

I lose track of the room, the nurses, the doctor. The pain swells like a wave crashing into the beach. I cannot stop it, cannot control it. I press my hands against my forehead and slip, again, through the void.

* * * *

I feel another scream welling up in my throat. I can't help but cry out as I come to, in the fetal position on the linoleum floor of my room.

Dominique is the first through the door.

"What is it? What's going on?"

I grab my skull and whimper. "My head. It's killing me."

My heart is racing, maybe even dangerously, but I am alive.

I am alive.

Dominique motions one of the other nurses to help me up and they get me into bed. I am useless, the pain so horrendous I can't move my limbs on my own. My whole body is reeling, shaking from distress and torment.

Dominique says something and the other nurse runs out of the room. I reach for her and she comforts me, rubbing one shoulder and holding my hand tightly. She is asking me questions, but I can't hear them. I can't process anything happening around me.

I could have died. I almost died.

Riaz and Strove both rush in the door with another nurse, who has a vial of something. Dominique draws some of the liquid out into a syringe and injects it into my arm. It doesn't take long before the pain becomes bearable and my muscles start to relax.

"Don't..." I try to form words through a thick fog. "Don't keep me away from Carrie. Please. I almost died."

Dominique reassuring me is the last thing I see as I drift out of consciousness.

- 25 -

KEEP GOING

Everything is calm. I feel a sense of contentment. A dizzy sort of undemanding awareness surrounds me. There is soft light, permeating my eyelids with a warm orange glow. I open my eyes, but the lids are heavy. It's as though there are magnets on my eyelashes, pulling the tops down to meet the bottoms. I struggle to keep them open despite the effort.

I try to turn my head. It, too, feels weighted and sluggish. I try to move my arms, but it's as if I've forgotten how to make that happen. I am thinking about raising my arms, but the actual action eludes me.

My attention is drawn to the doorway where the outline of a figure is coming towards me. I blink away my blurry vision and make out Dominique.

"Hey," she says kindly. "I'm glad to see you're awake."

I can hear her words, but they seem far away. Not unclear, but like I'm trying to listen to a concert through a door.

"How long?" I manage to say before the thickness of my tongue seems to get in the way.

"About twelve hours," she says, tucking a bit of blanket around my shoulders.

"Why…?" I start, but she shakes her head.

"None of that, now. The docs want to talk to you, but I want to be certain you can truly understand what they are saying. So I'm going to make sure you come out of this a little before I get them. Sound good?"

I nod.

"Okay," she continues. "You have some pretty heavy sedatives in your system, but they should be starting to wear off in the next couple of hours. I will be right here with you." She pulls over a chair and I see she has a magazine tucked into one pocket. "So," she begins, "I realize we don't have TV here, so I won't bother you with all that nonsense, but a good royal scandal is always fun, right?" She flips open the magazine and starts reading a salacious account of something some Duchess said that offended the royal family and the anticipated consequences.

Her voice is calming. It doesn't really matter what she is saying, though every once in a while, when she editorializes with little funny comments, I find myself smiling.

Slowly, over the course of two hours, the haze clears and I become more and more aware of what she is reading to me and what is going on.

She keeps a close eye on me, and after a particularly robust laugh at the rather public and humiliating demise of some Hollywood romance, she closes the magazine. "You ready for this?"

I take a deep breath. "No."

She sighs under her breath and raises her eyebrows. "I get that, honey. Let's try it anyway, though, huh?"

I manage a weak affirmation.

* * * *

Riaz and Strove are standing in basically the same position. Straight backs, hands clasped over file folders in front of them, with somber faces and determined postures.

"Ms. Donlan ~ " Dr. Strove begins, with Dominique standing quietly in the corner.

"Dr. Strove," I interrupt before he can continue.

He gives me a gruff scowl, but continues. "Your lapses are causing permanent, irreversible damage to your organs and, we fear, parts of your brain."

"Sure." This isn't news.

His scowl deepens. "You cannot continue to have lapses and survive."

"Wow. Way to really lay it out there, Doc." I don't have what it takes to be polite. "I think we all kind of knew that already, though, right?"

"Perhaps," he continues. "But I don't want you to think we are merely going to let you suffer. There are ways we can ease your pain while we mitigate the brain chemistry that is influencing your emotions, perhaps diminish the frequency and severity of your lapses and prolong your life."

I sigh. "So, let me get this straight. I can be me for the time I have left and then die or have less pain and no emotions and maybe live a little longer and still die."

"Ms. Donlan – " Dr. Strove continues but is interrupted by Riaz.

"We can keep you alive. We can prevent the lapses by preventing the extreme emotional response you suffer with your memories."

Memories. Not hallucinations, or episodes, or even lapses. So, he does think I'm crazy.

"You want to take away my emotions."

"Don't make it sound so dramatic. Controlling brain chemistry is not new science. We have made progress with serious mental illnesses by monitoring and modifying chemical imbalances. This is what I do," Riaz pleads. "Let me help you."

"But you don't know which chemicals are the problem, right? Or even if they are the problem?"

Riaz sighs, shaking his head. "It is our best option, and you are running out of time."

"Cut off all emotions, even though you don't know if that has anything to do with anything, and leave me – what – comatose? For the rest of my life? However long that might be." I shake my head. "I'd rather be me and die as who I am."

"If we hadn't found you, if Nurse Hughes hadn't been nearby..." Riaz shakes his head, fighting back tears. "You could have died. You almost *did* die yesterday!"

I remember the lapse, the transition through the ER on my way back to the here and now. "I know," I say apologetically. "But please, I need to keep my sense of self. I need to be me. What is the point of living life in a dream – in a false haze?"

"It is still life," Riaz counters.

"If you will not allow us a medical approach, there is nothing more we can offer you," Dr. Strove adds.

"Meaning – if I don't let you medicate me out of myself, I can't stay here?"

Dr. Strove looks at the ground and shakes his head. "If I cannot convince you to try and ease your symptoms, I feel this facility no longer meets your needs. We aren't equipped to handle the kind of care you will require."

Out of the corner of my eye, I can see that Dominique has crossed her arms and her posture is tense.

"I know I don't have a lot of options," I continue, "but I can't just be asleep. I feel like I have already slept through so much of my life. I didn't make friends even when there were wonderful people all around me. I didn't act when I should have, didn't tell people I loved them when I had the chance, didn't protect them when they needed me." I risk a glance to Dominique. She has a caring, somewhat sad, expression. "I just want to live my life." I try to control the sobs growing in my throat. "I need to be able to live my life."

"I'll draw up the paperwork to transfer you to a facility more suited to your... situation," Strove mutters, and walks out of the room.

Riaz looks crestfallen but doesn't offer any consolation or alternatives. He just leaves.

Dominique is still standing in the corner, tense. It looks like she wants to say something.

"Don't worry about me," I choke out, trying – and failing – to make her feel better.

"I think you need to come with me. Ms. Griffin is not doing well."

I burst into tears and she leaves the room, returning with a wheelchair. I wipe away the streaks on my face and blow my nose before allowing her to help me into the chair.

She wheels me the hundred feet to Carrie's room and all I can do is hold back sadness. I try to smile as Carrie's eyes flutter open. She manages an acknowledging head tilt back. It seems to take a great deal of effort, but it is accompanied by the smirk I have come to love.

Dominique leaves me with Carrie, closing the door behind her.

"Hi, kiddo," Carrie manages through heavy and strained breathing.

"Howdy, old lady."

She grins.

"Where have you been?" she wheezes. "Missed you."

Words are clearly becoming more difficult. For both of us, though for very different reasons.

"Just needed a break," I whisper.

She raises her arm, with effort, wiping away a tear from my cheek. It is one of thousands.

"Sorry." She shakes her head slightly.

"What? What on earth would you have to be sorry for?"

"You've lost so much…" She can't continue but I realize where she was going.

"I would never, ever wish I hadn't met you. You saved me. From the monotony of my wretched life, my self-pity, and just from myself. Don't you *ever* think that this whole thing wasn't worth it."

She looks at me, her eyes are still sharp and clear. "Life is worth it." Her mouth is quivering and her eyes glossing over.

I don't know what to say. She is dying and she knows it. There doesn't seem to be a way to comfort her. I don't want to lie, don't want to promise false hope, don't want to ruin what time she has left. I just want to be with her.

"Nightstand." She looks at it, with a slight turn of her head.

On it is a sealed envelope and next to that is the necklace she always wears – a gold chain with a sunflower pendant. I pick up the envelope and she shakes her head. "Later." She looks back to the necklace.

I pick it up.

"Open," she mutters.

Until now she has never taken it off. I examine it and find that it has a tiny clasp holding two halves together. I unhook it and swing the sunflower halves apart to reveal a tiny gold disk with the words "Keep Fucking Going" engraved on it. I burst out laughing and hold it to my chest. The laugh and the sobs are one big mess.

The beginnings of a chuckle bubble up in her throat, cutting short as she coughs again and gasps for air. I stand to go get someone and she shakes her head, instead pressing the button on a self-administered morphine drip.

She settles quickly, looking back to me after the pain has diminished. "Life…," she starts, slowly, "even with death…" She takes slower breaths, though they are shallow. "especially with…" Her words are barely audible now. "Life is worth it."

I take her hand. "Thank you," I say, clutching the necklace even tighter. "Thank you for everything."

She brushes a hair behind my ear, lets her hand cover mine, and then lets out a deep sigh, closing her eyes.

I rest my head on her stomach, clutching her, and watch her monitors. The alarms have all been turned off. Her pulse slows gradually, painlessly, and she drifts away. I stay with her. I tell her I love her. I watch her monitor as the last of the peaks and valleys diminish in size and frequency, then level out to a smooth line. I am with her when she dies and I feel completely and utterly alone.

- 26 -

CHOICES

Dominique checks on us several times throughout the night and gently pries me away from Carrie after the monitors have gone blank. Honestly, she probably let me stay longer than I should have. A kindness I won't ever forget.

I hold tightly to the necklace and letter as Dominique rolls me back to my room. She asks me if I would like something to help me sleep, and I shake my head. I want to feel this. I want to feel all of my emotions – in all their agonizing detail – because, I realize, this is what makes me feel alive.

I open the envelope, trying to read through thick tears, and I see only six words, written with an unsteady hand. "Thanks for the game. Keep playing." I cry myself to sleep, still holding the letter, with the gold chain wrapped around my palm.

* * * *

When I wake, I am more tired than I have felt in a long time. My body aches, the lump in my throat is thick and painful, and my head is pounding. My skin feels taut – stretched over tired muscles, brittle bones, and emptiness. My lips are dry, sticking together as I try to swallow – but I have no moisture left in my mouth.

I roll over slowly, seeking the water that Dominique has started leaving on the bedside table. I take a sip before I see him.

He seems small, withdrawn into the chair as though defeated, wounded.

When I see the collection of loose papers he's holding, I grip the letter more tightly, an irrational fear springing up that he will take this away, too.

It isn't worth asking him where he got the pages. They had been under my mattress. Any number of nurses could have alerted him when they were found.

I steady my gaze, waiting.

He takes a while to speak, working past his own emotions. "I'm so sorry for your loss."

I nod, still numb and empty, but not wavering from this conversation.

"How are you?" I prod gently, not taking my eyes off his.

"A bit knackered, to be honest." He holds up the papers and lets his hand fall back into his lap unceremoniously. "There is so much here," he manages.

I nod again.

"You should have told me. This information, this insane collection of data…" He pauses, clearly regretting his choice of words. "I mean, there is so much here that I could have used, to…" He shakes his head.

"To what?" I'm surprised by the clarity of my voice. Despite the hours of weeping and the lump in my throat, I am calm.

"This information." He looks back to the pages. "It demonstrates something I have never seen before. Something nobody has ever seen before." He runs a hand over his face. It looks like he hasn't slept in days.

"Oh, yeah?" I watch him steadily. "What's that?"

"Your brain is on a cycle. It's reliving your past moments in a contiguous stream. The times, dates, patterns, they all suggest some startling revelations about your brain." He looks up at me. "You are rerunning your life over and over again in precise increments. With this, we could anticipate your lapses, predict which traumatic experiences you were

169

going to relive, and medicate just those times. We could be proactive. We might be able to avoid sedating you all the time."

"No, you couldn't." I'm not trying to be cruel or disrespectful. It's just that it is not a true statement. "There is no predicting the lapses, even if we could determine the pattern."

"If? You mean you don't know? After all this," he motions to the papers again, "you didn't see it?"

"See what?" I sit up in bed, slowly leaning towards him.

"Eighty-four days. Your memory is repeating itself, like on a constant Möbius strip eighty-four days long."

Eighty-four days. How had he solved it? Had he seen all of this information as a puzzle? The Rubik's cube of my mind? Was it even possible?

"What does a Möbius strip have to do with all this?"

"Here." He picks up one of the loose papers. After evaluating it for a second, he rips a long strip down the side. "Think of this as your brain's timeline." He holds the strip up flat in his hands. "This is how we think of time – it starts on one side, moves ever forward, and we find ourselves at the end of the strip. Your brain, however…" He takes the paper and turns one end over once like he's making a twisted breadstick, and then loops the beginning and the end together. "Your brain isn't able to tell the difference between the present…" – he points to the outside of the twisted loop he has made – "…and the past." He touches the inside of the loop directly beneath where he pointed before. "Your brain is following this path, going from front to back in eighty-four day increments. To your brain, there is only one path, all the way around, and it switches from side to side, maintaining the chronological integrity of both timelines, maybe even all timelines, considering your lapse back to childhood."

Or the lapse through the ER, I think to myself.

His finger traces the outside of the loop and, without stopping, he ends up on the inside of the loop.

I can see now that it is a single line around both sides of the strip of paper. The way he has twisted it makes one continuous line that fluidly covers the entire outside and the entire inside.

"It is the strangest, most fascinating thing I have ever encountered in my entire career. It might be the most important discovery about brains in decades – this Möbius syndrome of yours."

I understand what he means. But I also understand that it isn't just my brain that's piercing through the strip, but my actions as well. Now I know exactly what I have to do. "What day is it today?" I feel my adrenaline starting to spike. If there is a pattern, a reliable pattern, I can go back. I can save her.

"It won't matter," he says, resigned.

"What do you mean? Please, tell me what day it is?"

"You'll be dead before the cycle is up," he says blankly, his face sinking.

"What?"

"These papers not only tell me some fascinating things about the way your brain is working, but they tell me what you think is happening. You think you are travelling through time." He shakes his head.

I can only stare at him. I can't deny it, because it is what I believe. And I can't lie, because I am no good at it and I don't want to. "You don't understand." I am trying to think of something to convince him to take me seriously.

"Actually, I think I do. Your sister died on October twelfth. According to your delusions…"

No.

"…to save her from the wreck, you would have to go back to her on one of the eighty-four-day markers. That means the next opportunity for you to act will be on June twentieth."

"And?" I can't pretend anymore.

"And you won't make it that long. If we don't work now to stop the lapses – altogether – you will die before then. Your heart or lungs or kidneys will give out. Your brain tissue will seize or harden or rupture. There is no way I can keep you alive that long without your help. To keep you alive, you will have to allow me to treat your brain the right way."

The right way. My heart sinks into my stomach. "You mean meter my emotions and…" I can't bring myself to say it.

"And treat your delusions. No matter what you choose, you cannot 'save' your sister, only yourself."

"Don't patronize me."

"I'm not." He shakes his head. "I am trying to save you. I am trying to help you see that you have to look out for yourself."

"You don't understand." I shake my head, swinging my legs out of bed.

"I understand you actually believe you can time travel." His shoulders move in a silent, despondent laugh. "I was so wrapped up in your case, in your story, that I didn't see how…confused…you had become."

"I changed my past!" My voice starts to rise, but I try not to lash out at him.

"Right," he says, "the burned arm. The thing only *you* can remember."

"I lived with it my whole life! I am not making that up."

"I don't think you are making anything up, Taylor." Riaz leans towards me, holding my gaze with his. "I think you need help. I think tragedy and loss and your accident have confused you."

I wipe new tears from my eyes. "Of course you do."

I lower my feet onto the floor to stand and face him. He leaps out of his chair to try and catch me, though I am not faltering.

"You don't have to save me." I glare at him and he retracts his outstretched arms. "I will figure this out on my own."

"Unfortunately, I don't think you can." He gathers the papers up and starts to leave.

"Wait! What do you mean?" I confront him.

"Dr. Strove and I believe you will be better off in a facility that can treat your mental illness as well as your physical breakdown."

No, no, no! My knees buckle under me. He drops the papers and catches me just before my knees crash into the floor.

"Careful, now," he says sweetly.

"How can I prove it to you?" I beg.

He shakes his head. "I am not going to feed into your... add to your confusion. Ms. Griffin should have known better. I care too much about you to do that."

He means delusion. I can feel my control of the situation slipping.

"Just, pick a number," my mind is racing. "Pick a number between one and a thousand and I'll write it down and put it in a drawer."

"You don't have a drawer," he says calmly.

"I'll scratch it into the wall, then." I can hear my desperation, but I can't remove it.

"You need to stop this."

It won't work. I can't carve a number into the wall without going back and I can't go back without knowing the number, which means the number won't be on the wall yet. I haven't changed it yet.

"Okay, no, you're right." I try to mollify him. "I just need to calm down and figure this out."

"Taylor." His voice is kind and gentle. His arms are still steadying me from my near fall.

I wrap my arms around his neck and pull myself closer to his body. At first he just lets me hug him, his arms wide. Then, slowly, he closes his arms around me and holds me.

The emotion of everything – of losing Carrie, of Riaz losing faith, of losing my freedom and maybe even my mind – is too much for me. Everything is suddenly so clear. My body starts to tingle and I can feel the hummingbird thump of my heart growing heavy. My lungs are tight and straining. I understand that I won't survive, but if I can just have one more lapse, one more chance to save Syd, it would all be worth it.

I pull my head back just enough to kiss him. He doesn't return it at first, and then falls into it just as I do. It is the most wonderful kiss I have ever had. His lips are soft and firm, his arms tightening around me just enough to lift me slightly up to meet him. His hand in the small of my back spreads out as his other hand pulls me in tighter. I hold the back of his head, embracing as much of him as I can. It is a passionate kiss; it is everything I had thought kissing him would be. But it cannot last. As quickly as it starts, it's over. We both pull away slowly. He runs his thumb over my cheek lets out a deep sigh.

"I'm sorry," I say, as he starts to shake his head and cradle my chin, "but I think I need to go now."

"What?" He looks at me questioningly, with a sweet gaze and his gentle smile. After a brief second, a look of horror crosses his face.

I feel the pull of the lapse straining my organs, as if I'm being crushed by some slowly increasing pressure.

He is speaking to me and his voice sounds so lovely with his beautiful accent, even though it is tinged with fear and distress.

I close my eyes and wait. I can hear him calling my name – screaming it, even – but it rustles my consciousness like a breeze through the tops of the trees. It seems it has always been floating around, swirling this way and that, at the edges of my mind – the lovely, desperate voice of love and loss.

The dizziness and pain start first, and then I am drawn through the whirlwind and thrown into another me from another time. I fall to the ground, overwhelmed more than usual now, as I realize the lapses, which have become more home to me than my Riaz reality, are pulling me apart – the present and the past fighting a war that – one way or another – must come to an end.

"Did the sidewalk jump up and bite you?" Aaron mocks as he helps me up to my feet.

"Of course it did," I manage, glad to see a friendly face.

174

There is no Christopher around, no Sydney, no drama of any kind, no issues that I can remember. It's just an early evening with Aaron, the only drama the fact that I have apparently tripped on a curb.

"Where are we going?" I turn towards him.

He looks at me with mild concern. "We decided on curry, remember?"

I do remember. This is the night Aaron and I decide to go pick up dinner so that we don't have to pay the delivery fee. I look up, remembering how we were caught in a sudden downpour, and I drag him under an awning in front of an apartment complex.

"Um, why – " he starts, laughing.

"It's going to start raining," I cut him off, watching the sky with contemplative reserve. I think I can still hear Riaz, maybe even an alarm or two or other voices, but it's as if all of it is coming from the wide and darkened sky.

"Yeah, I don't think so. There was, like, a three percent chance of rain today." He steps out onto the sidewalk to prove his conviction just as the first few drops pelt him and the surrounding pedestrians.

I can't help but smile from ear to ear. He runs back under the awning. "How did you do that?" He shakes his head a little and water droplets spray onto me.

"I can tell the future," I say, swallowing hard as a lump forms in my throat.

"Oh, really? What is my future, Madam Oracle?"

I turn towards him. "You're going to fall in love with my sister," I say with complete faith. "And you are going to lose her to a douchebag if you don't say something as soon as you realize it."

His face drops a little, shock spreading over his features.

"Oh, so you already are in love with her? Call her right now and tell her," I say, smiling.

"I met her like a week ago, Tay."

"Doesn't mean I'm wrong," I tease. "Go on. You won't regret it, I promise."

"Let's... just go and get dinner." He pulls up the collar of his coat and starts walking towards the restaurant.

"I'm dying," I say to him without really meaning to. My heart, tangible in my chest, is straining under the weight of so many lives lived, so many loves lost.

"What?" He looks at me with raised eyebrows and a smirk. When I simply smile and turn to him, his look changes to concern. "Tay, what's going on?"

"It doesn't matter," I say, taking a deep breath – slowly, as it is becoming more difficult. "I am dying, and the only thing I want in this whole world is for you to end up with my sister and for me to know that you will both be safe and happy. So, you have to do it."

"Ah," he says, the disbelief returning to his face, accompanied by some annoyance.

"Christopher will try and run her life, he'll hurt her, marry her, cheat on her, and get her killed. But you won't."

My veins throb with the struggle of keeping me alive and alert and *here*. My stomach is knotting up with grief and stress and pain. I am not afraid, though. I am finally calm.

"I know he's an asshole, Tay, but that's a hell of a leap."

The tendons and cartilage in my joints begin to ache. It's as though I am being stretched – drawn like taffy through a pulling machine, caught between whatever was then and whenever is now.

The constant is harder to hold onto now. My sense of self seems to be disintegrating along with the marrow in my bones. I can feel all of it. The details are starting to slip away.

But the constant has never been me, I realize. The constant is Sydney.

"I don't have much time," I continue to Aaron, though I still gaze up at the darkening sky as the sun sets beyond the heavy cloud cover. "He will marry her and he will hit her, and I will try and save her from him. I will pack her up in the middle of the night, drive her away from him, but he'll see. And he'll follow us and I won't know what to do."

The pedestrians on the street are now running to get out of the deepening rain. Thick drops falling onto cars and awnings and splashing back up into the air as a fine, permeating mist. I am as aware of each drop as I am of each cell of my body – like they are one in the same, spreading out in this moment to form a singular, ethereal presence.

I continue describing what will happen.

"I'll be so afraid – for her, for the *three* of us – I'll try keeping tabs on him. Without even thinking about it, I'll watch him in the rearview mirror and run a red light."

"The three of you? Tay, what are you even talking about?" Aaron sounds worried.

I cannot be bothered with his emotions. "I will run a red light. I ran a red light and a big, effing SUV crashed into us."

Was that then or is that now?

I look to Aaron for clarity, but instead I find his petrified expression. It's okay. I still have a moment.

"I won't be able to stop it," I tell him. "And I will have to live with it, forever, until it kills me. And it will. It is." Tears are streaming down my cheeks, but I am completely calm. I can feel little pinching sensations all throughout my body, like tiny tendons snapping.

Aaron looks horrified, but I find I'm content for the first time in a long time. "You will be great together. You are two of my favorite people. But you have to call her now, Aaron. Please, call her now."

I step backwards out from under the protection of the awning and twirl out into the rain. I dance like Syd danced on that long ago Fourth of July – independent and free. It seems fitting.

Each raindrop feels like a tiny bit of new life, of a new chance for me to do something right. I miss the rain. I miss the smell and getting tiny droplets forming on the outside of my wool coat. *Why do I miss the rain?*

My body is now covered in tiny explosions. Small sinuous connections shattering between realities. I can't go back now. It is so clear to me. I can feel the future ending, the me of then stopping. There are small surges of pain through my chest that I associate with lightning. Icy liquid spikes through my veins, but the coolness of it passes quickly. It's the sweet sobbing coming from the sky that I think I will miss most. A voice wracked with pain, but softened over distance or time. Or distance and time. I know that voice – filled with agony and loss and desperation. But soon, the voice gets lost in the rain.

It is getting much harder to breathe, but I am not worried.

"Call her," I say once more, looking at him. I reach into my pocket and find my phone. It feels so strange. I have completely forgotten what it was like to have a phone all the time. I open it and click on her number, handing the ringing phone to him.

The rain seems like it is falling more slowly. But everything is so beautiful. Aaron is calling her, speaking to her. It doesn't even matter that he has a concerned look. No matter what, this changes everything. They will save each other, make each other happy.

The pain is almost euphoric. It reminds me that not only am I alive in this moment, but it is different than what happened that night. Different means hope. Different means that she has a chance.

I throw my arms out and spin like I did as a child, letting the rain cover me and wash me away.

- 27 -

BEGINNINGS

The light is bright white. Clear and clean.

The silence is comforting.

It is finally over.

I take a deep breath, surprised to find the sensations of breathing that I remember.

I blink my eyes open and look around. What I had assumed was an ethereal white light seems instead to have been induced by some drug or other that has dilated my pupils significantly.

I am in a tidy, sterile room. Another hospital room, most likely, but I am not familiar with this one. When Marnie comes in, my breath catches in my chest.

The look on my face must concern her, so she comes over right away, "Welcome back," she says, helping me sit up by tucking a pillow behind my head.

I'm too tired to weep anymore. The irony of her statement is unbearable. The tears flow freely, unstoppable.

"Oh, hang on now!" Marnie takes my hand and sits on the side of my bed. "You're going to be just fine."

"No, I won't," I whisper.

"What was that?" She smiles at me, trying to comfort me, but I just want to die. I thought I had died. I thought my nightmare was over.

"You're awake!"

I can't let myself look. I have been dragged through this horrible condition, this Möbius syndrome, too many times. I've heard her voice too many times only to lose her over and over.

"Is she okay?"

Marnie looks to the voice. "She's going to be fine. The doctor thinks she was just dehydrated, which caused her to faint. The bump on her head after that was why we wanted to keep her under observation for a couple of days, to be sure she didn't have a concussion or any other internal damage."

I only hear part of this. Sydney is standing right here, talking to Marnie. She is biting her lip in her wonderful, nervous way and it is the most beautiful thing I have ever seen.

"There's no reason to be nervous," I whisper.

I did it. I changed my past, and Sydney's future. I know for sure, because these two women never met.

I swing my legs out of bed, even with Marnie's hurried insistence that I stay down. But I have Sydney in my arms before Marnie can stop me. She hugs me back, returning the vigor of my embrace.

"I thought I lost you," we say in unison, and immediately burst into simultaneous sobbing laughter.

In no time, we are ugly crying, with snot dripping down our noses and our red eyes spilling waterfalls of tears. Marnie helps me get unhooked from everything and Syd and I wait for the doctor.

Aaron comes in bearing sandwiches for himself and Syd, but he gladly relinquishes one to me when he sees I'm up. We hug briefly. He glances at Syd and her shy but coy smile tells me they have connected. He slips out to go and grab another sandwich and Syd and I talk, just like we did as girls. Both crying, both relieved the other is okay.

"So you and Aaron?" I say, tears of joy still coming.

"Is that okay? I thought you had a thing for him."

I crinkle my nose, embarrassed. "I did, too, but then I fell for someone else."

"Do tell!" Syd takes my hands in hers and I shake my head.

"He isn't around anymore."

"What?" She shakes her head. "You have got to stop falling for unavailable or completely unworthy guys."

"Yeah, I think I will. And you are going to stay away from that Christopher guy, right?"

Sydney grimaces. "After coffee the other day, when you were so adamant that he was – "

"An asshole," I finish for her.

"Yeah, well, after that I pulled back a little. Then, I was supposed to go to dinner with him, he insisted, but Aaron called, from your phone I might add, and he was really freaked out and I rushed over and met him at the hospital. Anyway, in my hurry I forgot to call Chris to cancel and he left this really nasty voicemail. I hate to admit it, but you were right, he was kind of a jerk."

"Kind of," I manage without too much trouble. He's out of the picture, that's all that matters.

- 28 -

LOST AND FOUND

I look at the piece of paper where I have scribbled the address. The street number is 632. I look up and see the building in front of me is 633, so I turn around. The building I'm looking for sits across the street, tucked between larger buildings on either side. It's small and simple, well maintained. A park is visible behind it through the space between complexes.

I wait for the traffic to clear and jog over. Once I'm on the sidewalk, I tuck my hair behind my ears and smooth my coat down at the waist. In the lobby I inquire at the reception desk and follow the directions I'm given to a bay of elevators.

As I step out of the elevator on the fifth floor I'm faced with a plaque showing, by arrows, room numbers 501-510 to the left and 511-520 to the right. I check the paper again to be sure and head right.

I take a deep breath and straighten my coat and hair again, nervously feeling in my purse to be sure my gift is still there.

I knock lightly on door 520, feeling more nervous than I thought I would.

The door opens after a second and my breath catches.

"Can I help you, kid?"

I can't help but burst into uncontrollable, overjoyed laughter.

Carrie looks perplexed, but intrigued. "Do I...know you?"

"Not yet," I say honestly. "But I have it on good authority that you are an excellent card player."

"True." She crosses her arms in front of her. "And are you here to play cards?"

"Sort of," I say with a grin, pulling a box out of my purse and handing it to her.

"Exploding Kittens," she reads out loud. "I'm not familiar with this one." She hands the box back.

"Nope," I say, refusing to take it. "I'll play you one round of gin rummy for one round of Exploding Kittens. We'll teach each other."

"What on earth?" She shakes her head.

"Please, trust me. I know you don't know me, and I can't explain why I think we will be great friends, but I need you to give me at least an afternoon."

Carrie shrugs, wary but clearly intrigued. "Well, you look harmless. Come on in, then."

* * * *

It's been almost four years with no lapses. Since the tether broke – which is how I have come to think of it – I've been here, in this timeline, solidly. Nothing forward and nothing backward.

Sydney is doing really well. She is healthy and brimming with life and love. I see her and Aaron as often as I can, and I insist on coffee once a week. We are closer than we've ever been. The first few times we went out, I tried to find the homeless man who popped up in two lapses, but I can't find him. I thought maybe he was really reacting to me, but the more I think about it, the more I realize he did exactly the same thing every time. I just stepped into his line of sight. It couldn't have been me.

Once I got over that initial desire to find him, and find out if he somehow understood what happened to me, I just focused on Syd.

She keeps trying to set me up. I think she realizes that I am pining for someone I cannot have. So she has introduced me to co-workers and brothers of college roommates and even random guys she met and thought I might like. She is charming enough that everyone says yes, even me, and I end up in a lot of uncomfortable dinners. Or even nice ones, but I am not interested. I only do it to keep Sydney happy. She is still my constant, and I will do anything for her.

I looked for Riaz before I even looked for Carrie, but I couldn't remember his surname and the memories of that past future get fuzzier every day. It's as if they were all part of a very elaborate dream. Since those memories didn't happen yet, in this timeline, and since they won't ever happen, it is hard to grasp onto them and bring them to light.

Everything else is going well, though, so I try not to think about it too much.

After Aaron and Sydney moved in together, Carrie moved out of her retirement apartment to room with me. I have told her everything, and she took it all in stride. Skeptical at first, but willing to keep an open mind, and finally, convinced. Or so I like to believe. I made her get checked for lung cancer as soon as I could, and I guess that kind of sealed it for her. We caught it early and she diligently did her treatment – I made sure of that. She's in remission now, living it up as only Carrie can. She's a riot as a roommate, an unsubtle wing woman, and my best friend. But this time, not my only friend. She is a force for positive change in my life.

After a bit of aggressive encouragement, she convinced me to finish my degree, and she helped me get a grant to avoid the student loan debt. Once I had my MFA, I spent months in temp jobs while I tried to find my best match for a career. On a whim, I visited the office building where my Cubies work, and I discovered that the "fun office" where Adonis would write on the window with dry erase marker is a startup technology firm. I had gone up just to see what all these places were like, but once I was actually standing in the lobby of that firm, I ended up in a conversation that led to coffee that led to an interview and an offer of a temporary position. After a few months, they brought me on permanently and I've been with them ever since. Adonis is really Jordan and Everyman John is Steve. Oddly, Jasmine is actually Jasmine. I find it comforting to be with them every day, and I sometimes walk to the window to look down at the building across the way, the facility where I did and didn't spend so many months in grief and pain. I'm not ready to go back there to check it out, but it feels familiar despite everything.

I've even had some encounters with my Cubies in the office below ours, some more meaningful than others. Scruffy has become an unexpected friend. His name is actually Kevin, but I still lovingly call him Scruffy, which he doesn't seem to mind. Scruffy and Lady, otherwise known as Hannah, have been dating for about a year now. So, by this strange, serendipitous roller coaster that I have ridden, I've begun accumulating lots of friends. People to work and play with, and turn to. The circle is widening beyond just Syd and Aaron.

I mostly have my life on track. Those four years never existed for everyone else. I lived an entirely separate life and I don't pretend to understand it. But I have everything I want, with the exception of romantic love with a specific handsome doctor.

* * * *

I cut a thick strip of paper and curl it once sideways and then tape it, tip to tail. My Möbius strip concept landed me my first real graphic design gig. I set the twisted strip on my worktable and trail my finger along it, watching it go from one side to the other in a smooth line, over and over.

"What in hell are you doing?" Carrie comes in with a bag of groceries and sets it on the counter.

"Did you get more – "

"Mustard? Yes, I know how you hate sandwiches without mustard."

I smile. "Yes, I do."

"Put on a nice outfit, I'm taking you out."

"What? No, let's stay in tonight. I'm exhausted after this Gideon project."

"But you finished it this week, right?"

"Yes," I say, stretching my arms above my head. "Finally."

"Okay, then, all the more reason to celebrate."

"Hmmmm, you make a good point. Where are we going?"

"Dinner and a movie."

"So fancy." I mock a swoon and flutter my eyelashes. "I'm ready."

"Don't be ridiculous, put on something nice."

I look down at my work attire. "This is nice."

"I mean something sexy nice."

"Not again, Carrie!"

She waggles a finger at me. "I will get you a boyfriend one way or another, girl."

"Not before I get you one."

This gets her deepest laugh. It's one that I love more than anything, because it is a booming howl made with two healthy lungs.

"Wear that pretty little shirt that Syd got you, with your date night jeans."

"Alright, alright." I do as she asks because I know better than to fight with her.

In no time we are headed to our favorite sandwich shop for too-large subs and freshly made chips. The adjacent macaron shop is our next stop. We pretend we're taking them to the theater, but we eat all of them before we are three blocks away.

She drags me into the theater and waves her tickets. "What are we seeing?" I prod her.

"It's a surprise," she grins.

A mumbling man jostles my shoulder as he pushes past me and I drop the subject, distracted. She pulls me inside under the marquis before I have a chance to figure out where I knew the man from or look up to see the title of the movie.

Once in the theater aisle, I nearly run into a woman and quickly stabilize her popcorn with both hands before she can drop it.

"So sorry," I say, more to the popcorn than to her. Then, "Dominique!"

"Yes?" She looks at me without recognition. "Do I know you?"

"Sorry, yes, well, no. I mean…" I take a breath. "You were the nurse of someone I was really close to. I always thought you were great. And your manicure game is on point."

She smiles and, her hands now free, wiggles all ten of her fingers. "Well, thank you."

"Here." I hand her the popcorn.

"I'd be happy to do yours sometime, if you like."

"Yes!" I don't even hesitate. "I'll call you. I mean, are you still at the same facility…" I try and cover as Carrie hides her chuckle with an awkward pretend cough.

"I'm at the Cormorant Rehabilitation Center. I don't remember…" She is searching for where she might know me from.

"Oh, yeah, I don't even remember the name of the other one. I'll remember Cormorant, though." I wave awkwardly and walk away.

"Subtle," Carrie smirks.

"I don't often see people from then, you know?"

Dr. Strove stands and waves at us. I almost fall over.

"Dr. Strove," I start, "how did you…" Thankfully he doesn't hear me.

Carrie strides over to him, and it hits me. *Of course, they were friends from before*, I think to myself.

Carrie gives him a big hug and I can't help but think she is flirting with him. "You sneaky little vixen," I mutter under my breath.

"Perhaps we should let them sit together?"

I spin around, shaking my head in disbelief.

"Sorry, it seems my colleague and your friend are acquainted. I just thought maybe we could help the old codger out."

"Riaz," I barely whisper.

He blinks a little and studies me curiously. "I'm sorry, I don't believe we've met."

"No, of course not, we wouldn't have, um…" I'm beginning to babble.

Carrie comes to my rescue again. "Taylor, this is Riaz, the young doctor I was telling you about. Robert and I were just talking about how nice it would be if he and I could catch up, and how lucky is it that there are two seats together here, and," she looks around, "ah, two more down there. You don't mind, do you?"

I could strangle her, but I keep myself composed. "No, that's fine."

"We were just discussing that exact scenario." Riaz directs me to a seat and I nervously fold up my coat and place it on my lap.

"So, you're from out of town, right?" I can't think of anything else to say. If he isn't here for me, why is he here at all?

"Yes," Riaz confirms. "Dr. Strove had a patient with a form of epilepsy he found somehow remarkable and called me in."

"And is it?"

"I beg your pardon?" He leans closer to me to hear over the din of other patrons talking.

I instantly remember his smell, the way his biceps stretch his shirtsleeves, the feel of his lips. I catch myself before I lean over to smell his musk. "Is it remarkable, that epilepsy?" I'm struggling to get back on track.

"You know," – he looks around to be sure he can't be overheard – "it really isn't. I don't know what possessed him to call me, but I have to say I have been enjoying my stay here."

"How long will you be in town?" I ask, a bit breathless.

"I'm not sure yet. I took the semester off, so I have a bit of time to fill."

He looks around and a sudden realization strikes him.

"Oh, my god." He covers his eyes and shakes his head.

"What is it?" I follow his glance, expecting to find an ex-lover staring at him.

"I didn't realize today was today." He shakes his head. "I have been busy trying to figure out what to do with my relatively empty days, but of course I would forget something like this."

I see lots of couples in the seats and realize what he means. "It's Valentine's Day," I say. I look over my shoulder at Carrie, surprisingly hand in hand with Dr. Strove. She winks at me. "And," I declare, "we are here to watch *The Princess Bride*."

"Yes. Are you familiar with the film?"

I'm grinning. "It's one of my all-time favorites. My sister and I used to watch it together all the time."

"Brilliant! It's one of my favorites, too. I'm pretty sure I introduced my baby sis to it."

It's nice to hear him talking about Liyana again. We can talk about our sisters without all the pain. We can just be friends who have siblings.

"That's nice. You must be a great big brother."

"I don't know about that. I don't talk to her much these days."

I sigh. "There's still time to change that."

His gaze is searching. "Yeah, I should give her a ring."

I nod and he runs his hand through his hair. I always loved it when he did that – filling the empty space in the conversation.

To ease him back on topic, I exclaim, "I'm really excited to see it in the theater. I haven't seen it on the big screen since it came out."

"Me, too! Although today might be an awkward day to revisit it with a total stranger."

"Don't worry," I reassure him. "I imagine everyone will keep the snogging and canoodling to a minimum."

He gives me a curious glance. And then I swear I see him wink. "That would be a shame."

Acknowledgements

A lot of people were very supportive in the writing of this book. I would in particular like to thank the following people, though this in no way represents everyone who has supported me through the years.

Thanks to my irreplaceable beta readers - my brilliant sister, Jennifer, my always supportive mom, Barbara, my encouraging mother-in-law, Marlene, and my amazing and patient husband, Steve. You gave me the confidence to continue.

Thanks to my incredible editor, Julie. I don't know where I would be without you.

Thanks to Alix for enthusiastically supporting the idea of a trilogy even though it threw a wrench in our release plans.

And last, but certainly not least, a huge thanks to my sons who supported me during a long and trying pandemic and found ways to entertain themselves so that I could write. I love you both to the ends of the universe and back.

Be sure to keep an eye out for the continuation of the

MÖBIUS SYNDROME TRILOGY

Book 2

REACTION

AVAILABLE JULY 6, 2021

To be sure you are kept up to speed with all the news and promotions for Raven and Quail Press, sign up for our email list on our website:

https://**raven**and**quail**press.com/

- 1 -

THE WEDDING

This is the perfect day.

Having relived, repeatedly, my sister Sydney's wedding to an abusive narcissist – and thinking each time that I couldn't change the outcome of her struggle and death – I never would have thought that I would enjoy a wedding ever again.

Especially not her wedding.

Of course, this isn't the *same* wedding that I returned to during those long months of lapses and medical issues. This is new. This is something I haven't yet experienced, and I couldn't be happier.

There are, of course, similarities. After all, Sydney planned them both. For instance, my dress is a similar shade of pale lavender, but it's more fluid, less stiff. That seems fitting to me, seeing as how Aaron, the groom this go-around and one of my best friends, is not a stifling influence but a freeing one. There are also fewer bridesmaids and groomsmen. It is a smaller affair overall, actually. The location is the same, but this ceremony isn't about proving anything to anyone. The last one, the wedding to Christopher, seemed more concerned with prowess and trophies. It was black tie, which only functioned to force some of our friends, Syd's and mine, to stand out in the crowd of Chris's wealthy colleagues.

But now, *this* sunset ceremony is about love. Instead of two hundred chairs crammed onto the small bayside lawn, there are fifty. And instead of the majority of the guests being on the groom's side, the guest list is about even. You see, Syd and I have been on our own since our parents died. We kept each other afloat and alive, but that kind of loss leads to reservations with new relationships. It's the problem of not wanting to love for fear of more loss. But I have learned that not loving at all is far more traumatic.

So this balanced ceremony is perfect. I have not lost my sister – neither to an overbearing husband nor to an untimely death – and I have the chance instead to see her truly happy. The fact that at one time I thought Aaron was my soulmate doesn't mean I lose him, either. His role has changed, that's all. He is still one of my best friends. And he is perfect for Syd.

Besides, I found what I wanted elsewhere.

I grin like the Cheshire cat when Riaz enters the room, searching the crowd for familiar faces. His eyes light up when he sees me and I wave him over to the bar where I have been standing, breathing in the wonder of the day.

"There you are," he says in his delightful British accent as he approaches. He stops beside me and looks down at his sleeves, fiddling with his cufflinks. "I swear these things are bloody irritating."

He stops suddenly upon seeing all of me, taking a short breath before smiling broadly and gesturing to my dress. "You look ravishing."

I perform a small curtsy and nod to him. "Why, thank you."

"My pleasure," he says. Then he stretches out his arms with a sheepish look. "Can you help me with these?"

I laugh but pull him closer to me so that I can adjust and refasten his cufflinks. "Better?" I ask.

"Much," he says, straightening his jacket on his broad shoulders and lightly tugging each sleeve to find a measure of comfort.

I lace my hand around his arm and rest my head appreciatively on his shoulder as we look around the room. "Thanks for doing this." I stand up on my tiptoes and kiss his cheek.

"Wouldn't miss it." He places his hand on mine, giving it a squeeze as he looks down into my eyes.

The crowd is milling about, eating hors d'oeuvres, drinking wine, catching up with old friends and making new ones. I see a friend of ours across the room, and I smile and wave. She waves as best she can, but her arms are full of a bright and bubbling baby girl.

"I'll be right back." I start to pull away from Riaz, but he clamps his hand down over mine and gently pulls me back.

"Please, don't abandon me."

I'm surprised. "Dr. Choudhury, are you trying to tell me you're shy?"

He straightens up, a bit of a blush in his cheeks. "No," he lies. "Just not entirely comfortable with a room full of strangers to *me* who all seem to know *each other.*"

I press my lips together to avoid laughing and pat his arm reassuringly. "You are the most charming man in the room; you'll be fine."

"If I were so charming, why would you want to leave my side?"

I laugh. "Touché. Come with me then and be my arm candy."

"Your what?" He is barely paying attention to me, his gaze roaming around the room.

"Never mind, just come along."

I gently pull him towards my friend Michelle. She looks the same as she did at the wedding I remember, and I have to remind myself that it never happened to everyone else here.

She adjusts the little wiggler in her arms and gives me a side hug.

"You look amazing!" I tell her. I hug her close, glad that she, and everyone else, is able to witness something truly wonderful.

"You too!"

The baby gurgles and laughs a little, pulling on her mother's necklace.

"And who is this?!" I wiggle my fingers out towards her. "Phalanges!" I say before tickling her belly. I hear Riaz chuckle behind me.

"This is Olivia!" Michelle hands the little girl over to me without hesitation. She's all flailing arms and legs in an adorable pink jumper and tiny shoes.

I am instantly in love. "You are just the belle of the ball, aren't you?"

A handsome, though tired-looking man comes over with two glasses of wine. "Here you go." He hands Michelle one.

"Oh, thank god." She takes a deep sip, then looks at me as though she thinks I might be judging her. "Don't worry, I pumped before we left the hotel." She suddenly seems to realize Riaz is standing beside me and her cheeks flush a brilliant pink. "I am so sorry! I don't even think about stuff like that!"

I can't help but laugh. "No worries. Dr. Choudhury is familiar with how bodies work."

Michelle sighs in relief and her husband laughs. "We don't get much sleep," he explains.

"Well, who would want to sleep when such a beautiful girl is begging for attention?!" I can't take my eyes off Olivia.

Suddenly, her expression sours a bit.

"Uh, oh!" Michelle's husband hands her his wine in a hurried gesture and grabs Olivia, turning her away from me just as spit-up dribbles from her chin and onto his jacket. He sighs. "Better me than you," he says to me, smiling.

"Oh, no! Rob, I'm so sorry!" Michelle is trying to use her cocktail napkin to clean him off. She turns to me. "Syd said she didn't mind the baby coming, but I would be mortified if she ruined your dress."

I shake my head. "She can't ruin anything, and I am glad your whole family is here. I don't think I've ever met…Rob, is it?" I hold out my hand.

Rob adjusts Olivia onto his hip, holding her with one arm and making sure her head is aiming at his already soiled shoulder. He extends his other arm and takes my hand briefly. "Yeah, Rob," he confirms.

"I'm Taylor. It's a delight to meet you. And thank you for the quick save."

"It's what I do," he says, faux-enthusiastically. "I'll go get the diaper bag."

"Ditch the jacket, if you like," I call after him. "It's a relaxed affair."

"I just might do that!" he says over his shoulder.

Of course, I am thrilled that Olivia and Rob are here with Michelle. At the wedding-that-wasn't, Christopher refused to have kids and even limited the plus-ones so as to fill the room with people "of consequence." I shake my head to get rid of the bad memory and introduce Riaz more formally to Michelle.

We talk for a bit before she heads over to where Rob has snagged a seat in the back of the rows of chairs.

Riaz seems to have relaxed a bit.

"That wasn't so painful, was it?"

"It does help that they were the ones embarrassed," he says jokingly.

"Oh, I know! Poor Rob."

"It's what babies do, or so I'm told."

The string quartet near the front of the lawn starts tuning their instruments and I realize I've left my sister alone too long.

"I have to get back to Syd, so you're going to have to be a big boy and stay here by yourself."

"Ha, ha," Riaz says dryly. Then he tangibly relaxes his shoulders. "Oh, thank god."

I follow his gaze to see that Carrie and Dr. Strove have arrived. Riaz catches their eyes and waves.

"Thank you for the brilliant escort," he says, bowing slightly over my hand to kiss it in mock formality.

"'Twas my deepest pleasure, Your Grace," I say in my best British accent.

He shakes his head and laughs. "I never should have watched *Bridgerton* with you."

With that, he leans in to kiss my cheek and then heads off to Carrie and Strove while I return to the small cottage where Sydney is getting ready. For her, it's the first time she's been a bride. For me, this room is too familiar. Too painful. But I am trying to see it through new eyes. Through hopeful eyes.

"Where have you been?" She's fretting over everything – adjusting her veil, pulling up her bodice, smoothing down her skirt, then pulling the bodice up again.

"Oh my god, Syd, stop fidgeting!" I take her hands in mine and turn her towards me. "Today is going to be perfect. Everything is perfect. You're perfect. Aaron is perfect. I'm obviously perfect."

This gets a laugh from her and she starts to relax a little.

"Okay, Crazy," I say, calmly, "deep breath." I look her in the eyes and take a long slow breath to demonstrate. On the second breath, she follows along.

"Right. Better."

She closes her eyes and I can see her shoulders relaxing. "It is perfect, right?" she says.

I don't even have to say anything back, I just smile and nod and her face lights up.

"Who all is here?"

"Well," I say as I guide her to a chair for final touch-ups. "Your work friends…"

"More like my Zoom friends," she interrupts while freshening her mascara.

"Yes, them," I continue. "And Uncle Paul…"

"Oh no!" She looks up at me in the mirror. "Any bad jokes?"

"Undoubtedly," I grimace. "My work buddies…"

"Is Jordan here?" She smiles with a devilish look.

"Yes, why?"

"Because that might explain why my bridesmaids keep slipping out for refreshments."

I cackle unintentionally. "I used to call him Adonis, before I met him."

"Fitting," she grins, "go on."

"Carrie, Riaz, and Strove, of course. Oh, Michelle is here with her baby girl and husband!"

"Oh, yay! She asked me if she could bring them and I told her, 'What kind of person would say no to a baby at a wedding?' She seemed surprised."

"Well, I agree with you. That type of person would have to be a real monster. Anyway, she's adorable."

"Speaking of adorable, did Kevin come?"

"You mean Scruffy? I haven't seen him yet, but I hope so. I think that he and Hannah are getting pretty serious. Maybe this will convince them to take the next step."

"Will you stop playing matchmaker with everyone?!"

I fake offense, putting my hand on my chest. "Whatever do you mean?"

"You're ridiculous."

"Yeah," I smile. "But I think Kevin and Hannah are both happier for it. And, let me think, did I introduce anyone else…?"

She glares at me in the reflection. "Fine. You did *technically* introduce Aaron to me, but I was bound to run into your roommate at one point or another."

One of the other bridesmaids comes in and tells us that the music has started.

"Are you ready?" I hug her from behind, looking at the two of us side by side. I notice her engagement ring is still on her finger. "Do you want me to hold that for you?"

"What?" She looks down at her finger and shakes her head. "I'll just move it when I need to. Or, is that bad?"

I've done this before. I use my most informational voice. "Tradition dictates you shouldn't wear it on your left ring finger during the ceremony, but you can wear it on your right hand, if you want to."

"How the hell do you know that?" She starts trying to jimmy the ring off her finger.

I look around for a bottle of hand lotion. It isn't in the place I expect it to be, but that only makes me smile. Things are different this time.

"It's really stuck on there!" She squinches up her face while trying to tug the ring off.

I find another bottle and hand it to her. "Don't tug; you'll make your finger all red."

"Oh, thanks." She puts a little lotion on her finger and the ring slides off without too much trouble. She quickly switches it to her right hand. "You're really on it today."

My sister smiles at me and rubs the remaining lotion into her hands.

I nod and straighten up.

"Let's do this."

Printed in Great Britain
by Amazon

25388031R00116